To be an outcast is to be the pillar of a new beginning.

Do tell.

Table of Contents

Rain drops splattered the life-ridden battleground. On the cold, cloudy night, the eyes of the fallen were colder than the droplets on their shoulders. The cold air wore a scent of blood as atop the valley of death stood two men on a cliff. Ones helmet to the side, as his knees finally gave out against the weight of the world.

"It's over. Give up your helm. Face your death honorably."

The man chuckled, "There is no honor in death. There is only honor in strength. Only honor in power. As long as I live—I'll never bow down to another man."

The man forced his legs to stand, as his knees crackled with the whims of defeat.

"I'll die as I lived—prideful—with something to prove. I'll fight till my last breath. You should know that better than anyone else."

The man struck his spear forward. As it was parried, a sword struck through his body. His spear fell over the cliff, as his body followed soon after.

1

Chapter 1: The Outcast

To be different is the essence of change. To be different is to stand against the waves, and refuse the tide.

I was born into solitude. A seven-foot purgatory of dirt and stone. A heavy scent of sulfur and deafening tranquility, my only companions. For years on end, I would sit in silence, never setting sights on another soul. It wasn't all bad though, I had the insects and other critters, alongside the deep-voiced man to keep me company.

Humans fear what they cannot control—for that reason, they fear the dark. Cowardly and weak, they dare proclaim themselves at the top of the food chain—assuming strength through delusion.

The deep-voiced man taught me everything I knew. From the language of Greek, to what it means to be a man. As far as I knew, the world I was born into consisted of dirt and dust. The outside was unknown, just a mystery I craved to solve. I spent years inside the ditch tortured by the laughter and the festivities outside, and the silence and fear that followed every night. I was forgotten by the world. The deep-voiced man remembered me. He was sunlight, in a world pillaged by darkness. Against the threat of my existence, he saw beyond his fear. He didn't see a powerful beast; he saw a child. Lost, confused, born into a world without family. He rose against the tide and stood amongst the breeze.

It's amazing what a different point of view could do. It could change the conversation.

However, as all things mortal, nothing is forever—and as the world would come to understand, there is no point in forever.

Having been in this box for so long, I had given up on escape. The idea of freedom was arbitrary and impossible as if a finish line that only got further with every step. I had grown to understand I would live out the rest of my days here. Interrupting my skulking, was a sound of mumbled words mere feet away. Shocked and afraid, I grew to realize that Dimitris would never be so careless as to announce his arrival—for if I could hear it, surely the guards would too. I was a monster in the eyes of the villagers. Other than Dimitris, the deep-voiced man, I had never had a visitor before. So, it sent shivers down my back as I heard, for the first time in eighteen years, a child's voice. I wasn't sure what to even imagine; *would they be tall or short? Fat or skinny? Red, maybe blue?*

"Euripides, you know what Father said about the trap door!" A voice echoed from the top of my cage.

"I don't care Yiannis. I need to see."

After eighteen years, I heard the trap door click. Ironic how such a tiny, trivial sound changed my life. A mute sound, almost—yet hollered. I was released, along with the dust trapped within. I tasted the bitter taste of dirt as it landed upon my pale white face. The trap door lifted, and in those few moments of agonizing wait, I relived the past eighteen years. From the tears to the anger, past the pain and the loneliness—I saw a bright light. Mystical, maybe even divine. It felt as if it was calling upon me—inviting me to the world—the same one that isolated me for so long. From the arms of fate, the face of a young child was revealed. A dagger of light and fresh air pierced through the darkened chambers of my past. I could feel the air getting lighter and smell the scent of sulfur slowly rotting away. Fear and uncertainty spoke lectures through his ocean blue eyes. His dark blonde hair rode the wind, as my palms reached for escape.

The kid threw himself back and darted past what I could see. With all my might and limited strength, I pulled myself out. I could feel my muscles stretch for the first time, an act of might, and a callous call for vengeance.

I heard the children scream in horror in the near distance. The obnoxious scream of a prepubescent child slowly faded away as the bright sun burned my decaying skin.

Terrorized for eighteen long years—trapped in a pit, my life decided by peasants. My anger and my agony fueled my roar. A roar that told stories of imprisonment, of pain, of despair. I was hidden away from the world for years. A strength I had never perceived to be possible invested itself within me. I felt heat. As if a flame that was long extinguished had been returned to me. The rightful heir to choice, to power, to voice—yet burdened by chains and inability. I was born anew. I fell to my back on the grass that surrounded my prison. I breathed it all in, the fresh air of the orange sky took my hand, while the cold breeze rode my long black hair welcoming me to the world, as the warmth of the sun erased the darkness of my cell. I was no longer forgotten. I was here. *I was alive.*

In the distance, I saw mountains rise past what I could perceive. I saw birds, I saw clouds—I saw orange deities brush the sky with a beautiful color that remarked a sunset. I felt a sense of discovery at that moment.

Finally, Freedom. I thought to myself as I sat up.

That is until a spear drove through my chest, relieving me of the air I was so fond of. I looked down to see the tip of a tough steel reflecting a crimson light.

Even so, no dagger, no blade, and certainly no spear could take my life.

The men of the village strung me up to a wooden pole in the center of their society. I was put on a pedestal for all to see for hours. My eyes, heavy, I listened carefully for there was a familiar voice shouting in the distance.

"He is a child!" Dimitris shouted, advocating for my life.

"He is a monster, Dimitris! You know why we must do this! Unless you wish to join him, step back!" A strong-voiced man demanded; a plea of worry resided in his golden voice.

"You are the monster Vassilios. Don't kid yourself. For years, you kept a child locked away from the world. Stripping him from his potential—stripping him from his—"

The tear of flesh interrupted the deep-voiced man. My one ally against a world of enemies.

"I will not tolerate incompetence."

His screams haunted my dreams for years to come.

I felt a warmth crawl up my body. A heat, unlike anything I've ever experienced. Red and yellow embers contrasted the dark, cloudy night. I wasn't sure what I was smelling, only that it made it difficult to breathe.

"Tonight, we'll dine knowing the sins of our past have been quenched! The Beast of Baylor dies!" The crowd cheered in response.

My tears could not extinguish the flames, no matter how deep. I stood there, burning, for the enjoyment and the relief of the people of Mizeria. The monster was finally slain.

Why were they cheering? What had I done wrong?

A dark, forgotten sound resonated inside my skull. A pure eternal rage made its way to the surface after years of imprisonment. I lost my voice as a child—and I'd never allow it to happen again.

Why were they cheering? What had I done wrong? I repeated as I gripped the pole I was strung to. I repeated as I heard the screams of my old friend blare in my ears.

My head was loud, and I couldn't stop the voices from hollering. I felt so much pain inside my heart that it overwhelmed the flames set upon me. My thoughts were so loud, I couldn't think—as if drowned in a sea of noise.

In an instant, I understood who, rather, what I was. They were right. I was a monster; I felt it inside my chest—the burning hate—the urge to burn every man, woman, and child in this godforsaken village. Even so, I was a monster that had yet to do wrong. I served the time for a crime I never committed—a crime I never got the chance *to* commit. However, if I am going to be called, controlled, and imprisoned like a monster, I figured I owed myself to live up to that title.

That's when I broke through my barrier. No, not the steel that held me to burn. A wall came crashing down inside my heart, and the fencing between right and wrong came crumbling down, allowing me a choice. I broke through my shackles, putting one foot in front of another escaping the embers set upon me, as the crowd screamed and fled in horror. The strength from before returned, although clouded by a crimson rage. My heart ached for battle. I felt time itself bend to my control. Every detail of the foreseeable battle was clear. The guards and their bronze swords, the men and women of the village fleeing, the rain falling on my shoulders. I roared yet again. One of hate, one of power and strength, and one of death. One of the beasts with nothing left to lose, the roar that precedes massacre, one only described as a banshee's scream. Death was imminent.

I drove my fist through the first guard's shield, as I plunged his sword through his gut. I smiled as I felt his last breath escape his body. His eyes fell still. His final thoughts disappeared before he was forgotten to history. Maybe he thought of family, maybe he thought of money, of success, of the potential he never could realize—but it didn't matter. This was the proverbial line in the sand. As I held his lifeless limp body, I knew I was responsible for the blood that stained my hands. I dropped him, his body landing in a pile of mud. Dirtying my worn-out tunic. I put an end to his reign of terror. His comrades would soon follow, and I knew I'd regret every step—but I finally had a choice. They drove me to this. I wouldn't stand idly by for the sake of bureaucracy. They took me from the warmth of safety and stuck me to the cold walls of my prison and that was unforgivable.

The adrenaline of the battle fueled my every step. The rush of the fight led my fists through many. Blood, sweat, tears, I no longer can tell the difference.

Before long, I stood atop the man they call Vassilios, a tall strong figured man. A maniacal smile took control of the pain—the misery—the despair of my existence. If I was a monster, so be it. I would reign hell upon this town. I drove his sword through his neck. His gurgled screams burrowed a canal through my ears. It was my sanctuary. Next to his lifeless body sat a single rose. Beautiful, alone, and tainted with the blood of my enemies. Its crisp red petals reminded me of a simpler time. Death—that's all I could think of at that moment. That was the only guarantee we had. In this world of mystery, death is our only friend. It would never deceive or trap us. It's not the end of the road, it's the ability to no longer follow one.

That's when it hit me. As if drilled into my brain was a memory.

It was cold. A gray sky signifies a dark day. Rain splattered all around me. My red eyes and their light warmed me against the sounds of death in the background. I saw a hand reach towards me, bloodied, weak, it looked safe. Its final strength is forced through sheer will alone. It dropped on top of my tiny chest after a sound of flesh tore.

I was picked up, my eye meeting another. White, mystical. It felt warm, yet deceiving as if contradicting itself with every thought.

Who was this mysterious man? What did this mean for me? Who am I?! I fell to my knees before the mountain of bodies I had built screaming for answers. *What was my name? Who did I belong to? Who was the white-eyed man? Where do I belong?*

I turned to the sky, facing the rain, my voice throbbing, sore after a night of battle. Rid of strength, yet filled with an emphasis of a distraught voice climbing to the surface.

I tried to remember, but it was fruitless.

Sounds of slaughter echoed in my mind as they drowned my voice in a distant realm. I couldn't think, but against the chaos that bounced from wall to wall inside my head, I heard coughs and a calling from across the courtyard.

He raised his hand to the sky, hoping I'd see it—the last resort, of his diminishing strength.

I ran to him, jumping into his arms. A stain of red found itself on my tunic immortalizing his unhinged spirit into the fabrics of the beige shirt, holding on so he may not leave me to be alone again.

"Son." He said past his fleeting strength.

"Dimitris. Don't go–please. Stay with me."

"I was afraid of this." He interrupted himself, coughing up his strength.

"Don't talk Dimitris—you need your strength!" He smiled in response.

"I can try to patch you up, let me see if I can find anything," I said, stuttering and standing up before he pulled me towards him.

"I had a sword drive through my gut. This is the end for me."

A tear drove down my face.

"This doesn't have to be the end for you too."

There was a silence before I continued,

"What do you mean? What can I do?"

"You can fight. You can fight till you have nothing left to give," He paused before continuing, "this world is evil. It'll try to take everything from you—but you need to promise me that when it inevitably does, you'll keep fighting."

Another tear dropped as my eyes were filled with grief.

"I promise Dimitris. I promise to keep fighting." I held his hand as I felt his strength wither away.

"My son died by a Spartan's hand. He gave up everything so he may fight for his nation. His final thoughts were of home I'm told, the one thing he wanted to protect the most. He was prideful and talented. Some amongst the army even went as far as to say he was a man turned God. He's long gone now. From his death, I learned what war was capable of. I could go out and avenge his death, but that would only leave another father without a son and another mother that died of heartbreak.

In my final moments, I ask you to take his name. I want you to fight for what you want to protect the most. Let my son's legacy live on through yours. I beg of you."

I nodded, another tear falling off my cheek.

I saw a smile form upon Dimitris' face as he looked to the sky,

"Thank you. Thank you for giving me another chance to be a father, Ollius. You'll grow to be a legend. You'll fight battles that'll take you back to this day, but you'll never forget your name now."

He went on to explain who I was. My origins before I was imprisoned. As a child, I was a prisoner of war. The fall of Sparta marked me for death. No matter how hard they tried, the townspeople could not kill me. Through countless blades, either from iron, or blessed by mages from distant lands. Not one can take my breath. Through heaps of poisons, and flames. Through endless submersions, no matter how deep, I survived.

Eventually, they gave up and just threw me in a pit, hoping I'd starve. As the menace of the village and a threat to the world, I was given the name of the Beast of Baylor. I was a legend, the boogeyman that every child feared. For that reason, the child freed me. To conquer his own fear. However, in doing so, he paved the path of my endless rage. A rage that would stretch far past this small town. A rage the world would come to fear.

That night turned into bloodshed, a massacre. I arrived at the village, a child. I left the village, a champion.

"Just remember, Ollius. You cannot move forward by looking backward. You'll only stumble."

Chapter 2: The Beast of Baylor

After Mizeria fell to my hands, the officials of Greece were puzzled as to who or what held enough power to wipe out an entire city's army in a mere evening. Some people called it a massacre; others called it an act of God. They were right on both accounts.

Nevertheless, the Beast of Baylor became the prime suspect, at least unofficially.

Fear stretched across the lands. My name rode across both Greece and Baylor in waves of fear. The investigators found my pit and the survivors of my onslaught. They told stories of a rabid beast tearing apart their city. Homes were burned to ashes, and guards and soldiers succumbed to a storm of a single man. They found books and stories about the tale of the Beast of Baylor. The baby that survived any dagger, any flame, enchantments by the greatest sorcerers of Greece. A mysterious captive, and a secret held together by an entire town. Officials found this hard to believe. Officially, the story of the Beast of Baylor has been ruled a hoax, just a bedtime story for children.

In a world filled with mysteries and unknowns, I struggled to find a place for myself. I was a felon, responsible for the death of Mizeria. My red eyes stuck out like a sore thumb. My abnormally strong physique did not help blend me in either. I spent an entire day roaming the streets for shelter—however, alone in a new world, with no friends and plenty of foes, it was hard to trust anybody. I made my way to the outskirts of town and found a cave stuck on the side of a cliff.

I approached the cliff, reaching for the first rock, I found that I pulled myself up quite easily. I was surprised. Earlier, after my escape, I could barely pull myself up out of the pit. It took everything out of me to do so. Now, it was second nature to me. My strength was overflowing. I could quite literally feel the power radiating from my palms.

Sooner than later, I found myself standing in the dark cave. It was shallow, more of a hole rather than a cave. I still searched within, hoping to find something to fill my stomach.

A couple of minutes later, I called the search. I had no choice but to go to sleep hungry, that idea was nothing new to me.

I spent hours planning out my next move. I wasn't good with people, to say the least. They didn't trust me; I didn't trust them. I was a Spartan without a home. I decided I would coast from city to city until I could find my father. Dimitris told me stories about him. There was almost an endless supply. I could recall a couple, for instance, the battle with the Hydra of Corinth. His journey through Greece. His battles, and his army of ten. The respect and fear he instilled within the good and evil of this world were unparalleled. He was a hero, a villain, anything he wanted to be. Dimitris was too afraid to say his name, therefore I never learned it. However, I knew the time would come when I'd reunite with him.

I sat at the edge of the cave, staring up at the sky. Swarming with stars, it was a beautiful sight. Dimitris told me about these stars. He wished I could sit alongside him, picking out different constellations so he could tell me the different stories. He could tell me about Mount Olympus' champions. He could tell me stories of the heroes of the past, stories of devastation, of success, of empathy. However, sorrow and loneliness were the only companions that sat alongside me that night. Looking up at the star-extensive sky the only thought that crossed my mind was, "I wonder if my father was looking back at me".

Dimitris had mentioned my father was of great importance. A man of great stature, and respect. Although, he would never tell me his name. Would he care enough to find me? Maybe this was a one-way relationship. Maybe that would be enough for me. Maybe that's all I needed.

Before dawn broke, I saw fire approaching the entrance of the cave. I stood up immediately—in an instant, I had my sword unsheathed. In another, I had it to the neck of the invader pressuring him off the cliff.

"You're here for my neck," I whispered.

"You're mistaken, please. Put down your sword." The mysterious man pleaded.

"Your name. Give me your name." I warned, deepening the blade.

"I'm with the Legion. I am not here to hurt you—"

"You speak as if you could." I interrupted.

"I am only here to recruit you, Son of Sparta."
The man said, "We share the same mission. We both
want to bring Greece to its knees."

A moment of silence echoed against the walls of
the cave.

"How can I trust you?" I responded.

"You're the one with the blade to my neck."
The man quickly said, with a hint of fear in his voice.
His conscious mind was unsure of whether fight or
flight is possible. His lungs were fearful of the last
breath. His neck, anxious of the blade threatening its
stability. A silence took over the room.

I lowered my blade, and as I allowed him to
move deeper inside the cave, the man tripped over
himself.

"How do you know I'm a son of Sparta, and
how did you find me?" I asked, suspicious and weary
of the answer.

The man awoke from his knees, "We are the
Legion. We are the last blood of Sparta. Eighteen
years ago, our homes were burned to ashes. Our

fathers and mothers perished at the hands of the Achaean League. We are the last warriors in a long-forgotten battle. Of our men, one is a talented sorcerer. He is responsible for locating you." The man recited, quickly and anxiously.

"The Achaean League? Dimitris had mentioned them before, who are they? Better yet, you still haven't even given me your name—who are you?" I asked, taking a step towards him.

"I am a Scout for the Legion, a connoisseur of Sparta's revival. I am Hermaeus of the Legion, but my friends call me Herm."

"Why seek me out? Why are you here?" I asked with my sword to my side.

"We need warriors. The Achaean League decimated our armies. We are the last remnants of Sparta. We need any and every able-bodied man." Herm responded.

"I've no idea of your true plans. Why would I trust you? I am a wanted felon; I just destroyed an army! The entirety of Greece is bearing down my neck." Pausing, before I continued, "That being said, I already dealt with my captors. I wield no hatred for Greece." I said as I sheathed my sword, turning away.

"You are a Spartan, are you not?" Hermaeus asked.

"I am," I answered, looking back.

"Where's your shame?! The Achaean League killed your parents. Slaughtered your people in cold blood. They raided Sparta, leaving it in debris. They took you hostage, forcing you into captivity for eighteen years!" Herm shouted while anger and sadness enveloped his voice.

"How do you know that? And I've already told you, I dealt with my captors. I forgave the town's transgressions and put down the dogs that stood in the way of my escape." I responded while I was getting ready to leave.

"Who do you think Mizeria was? Just a town responsible for your captivity? That was not on them, Son of Sparta. They were merely puppets. If you think you completed your mission, you are sorely mistaken friend."

"Herm. You reek of ambition. Although I cannot speak for your strength, your will speaks for itself. However, how am I to trust anything you say? You are a stranger after all. We come from two different worlds."

"Because I was old enough to witness it!" A silence preluded, "The inhumanity. The screams, the blood. The Dusk of Dawn. My entire family, from my baby brother to my grandfather were slaughtered in front of my eyes. I was only a child of four stuck in a closet. We may be strangers, true. However, our worlds collided years ago. We are both victims of fate. Lend us your sword, so we may strike down Greece to its knees. I beg of you Son of Sparta." Herm lectured, now back on his knees.

"It's funny. You claim to be a victim of hate— you claim *we're* victims of hate, yet you want to spread it. You want to use my arm to strip away sanctuary."

The cave fell silent.

"I'm sorry. I just simply cannot trust you. You walk in here expecting me to leave with you. You fall to your knees, begging me for help—but there's just something in your eyes that tells me not to believe you. You're hiding something—"

"You defeated an entire city!" Herm interrupted, slamming his fist into the ground below. "How am I to defeat you?" He asked, looking up into my eyes. His eyes were teary, brown, and desperate. His voice was shaking. In the deepest pits of his heart, an arm rose— one of hope, one of redemption. One of promise.

"Just come with me. You'll know it's all true once you see our fortress."

The silence of the cave returned.

"Hermaeus. Stand up." I offered him my hand.

"Because if I have to regret this decision, you will too," I said as I picked him up off the floor.

"Then we're in this together, Son of Sparta." Herm, now thrilled, responded as he shook my hand.

I held his hand, putting another atop,

"Ollius. My name is Ollius."

Herm smiled in response.

The journey to the Legions camp was treacherous. One of our many obstacles was, of course, hiding my face. As a wanted felon, responsible for the death of hundreds, I did not find myself to be welcomed in many places.

"Tell me about the Legion," I asked as we rode our horses towards camp.

"We're made up of the last Remnants of Sparta. We—"

"What does that mean? You mentioned it earlier in the cave. A Remnant of Sparta." I said as I looked back to the path.

"To answer that, you must know the truth of what Spartans actually are. It is no secret that Spartans trained vigorously for the entirety of their lives. From the moment they learn to speak, to the moment they draw their final breath, whether on the battlefield or on their deathbed.

Now, over the years, something interesting happened. You see, a sorcerer needs not only the skill to provoke incredible magic—but a sacrifice also. Something needs to be exchanged to produce any sort of magic. The stronger the sacrifice is, the stronger the magic is. Due to their high-intensity training over the years, and their selective breeding. The Spartan Warrior was changed. Not only did their body strengthen, but their blood did so too. Because of this new evolution, the magic that the sorcerers could produce was beyond anything the world has ever seen. Magic, so strong, that it was said to rival the Gods. A sorcerer could tear apart cities in mere moments using a single cup of Spartan blood. The Greek world saw this as a threat. Thus, Baylor created the Achaean League, and vowed to destroy every Spartan alive." Herm lectured.

"Baylor?" I asked.

"You've been stuck inside that cage for a while. Everything you see around you is Baylor. This entire realm we exist in. That rock, that tree. We live in Baylor."

Demetrius had never mentioned Baylor before. Apparently, it was the literal world we lived in.

"If their blood was so powerful, why not use it to destroy the Achaean League?" I asked, puzzled.

"You'll come to find out that the only thing more lethal than Spartan blood was Spartan pride. King Agesilaus refused to rely on magic to win a war of combat. He made the callous choice of prioritizing pride over blood. Literally, and figuratively." Hermaeus said as a wave of sadness took over his expression.

"You say they vowed to destroy every Spartan alive, and yet you breathe, alongside this Legion. How did you and the other Spartans escape?" I asked.

"During the ambush, Thomas, our camp leader, helped us escape. He was twenty at the time, and one of Sparta's top warriors. His combat ability and his vision were unlike any of the soldiers at the time. He saved me before they got to the closet." A silence took hold before Herm continued, "The rest of the Spartans were saved by either crazy good luck or their parents. It's thanks to the fallen that we have the talent we do."

As we rode our horses, I spotted a trio of trouble across the way. They wore dark clothing, and some even gripped a sword. They reeked of greed and envy. Their clothes of leather, and their blades of steel.

As we got closer, the men took note of us riding on our horses. One of the men crossed the road to the other side, as another stood in the middle, blocking our path.

We were surrounded.

"Sorry to be the one to tell you this, but there'll be a fee if you want to pass." The man in the middle said, who looked to be in charge. His arms crossed, and his eyes pompous and domineering.

"A fee?" Herm asked.

"Yeah. That'll be a hundred Reels." The man answered.

"Under whose authority?" Herm asked as he reached for his blade.

"The Kings."

"That's funny, I don't remember giving that order," I said as I smirked, hopping off my steed winking at Herm, signaling him not to make a move.

"You're bargaining for a lot. You sure you can back that up?" I asked before I pushed the man, sending him to the ground.

The man to the left swung his fist. I ducked and sent a jab towards his nose when I rose. He stumbled back before I punched him, knocking him off his feet. The other man tried tackling me to no avail. I locked my hands around his torso, slamming him onto the ground behind us.

Immediately, I turned around and grabbed the first man's blade before he could contact the back of my head.

I took his blade, throwing it to my side. I grabbed him from atop his skull and slammed him into the ground. I didn't stop till I could no longer feel him resist. He let out an exhale before I let him free. A distinct sound of wheezing blew with the wind.

"I am the King," I said as I mounted my steed, leaving the mess behind.

Hours later, we arrived at the Legions camp.

Pillars of stone guarded the entrance. A giant gate stood between us and the Legion's menacing quarters. Walls of stone contrasted by wood held together the last stand of Sparta. It was a fortress, armored by humanity's greatest warriors.

"Welcome Ollius. This is the Legion."

"You built this?" I asked in awe.

"It wasn't easy—but it's been eighteen years. While you've been in a cage, we've been getting ready for a fight back." Herm said, chuckling.

I turned my head to Herm, with a sour feeling in the back of my throat.

"Sorry.

Let's just go inside." Herm continued, stuttering.

Herm approached the giant gate and proceeded to shout,

"Ant! Open up! I've got a guest with me."

A voice joined Herm from atop the wall.

A man of thirty-five looked down at Herm. His hair was short and black, and a physique of strength and endurance, he wore a set of iron armor and looked to oversee visitors.

"Hermie! Have you caught another Remnant?"

"Yeah! Have Daniil fetch Thomas. He'll want to talk with this one personally."

The giant gate slowly opened, and as Herm led the way inside, I followed.

Inside the walls were barracks, armories, and a cafeteria big enough to fit hundreds of people. This wasn't just a fortress; this was a civilization. I saw kids run past me laughing, and their parents following soon after. I saw training grounds, homes, and other buildings.

This town was one of the biggest I have seen yet.

I followed Herm through the town. We passed dozens of men and women all armed to the teeth. I wasn't used to being around this many people.

"Don't be intimidated, Ollius. These are *your* people." Herm said, looking back at me.

"I'm just not used to seeing this many," I replied.

"Okay well, just don't tear apart this town." He said as he laughed.

"Seriously?" I replied, defeated.

"Lighten up Ollius, we're almost there," Herm replied, grinning.

I continued to follow him, my eyes, however, followed the sounds of laughter and ecstasy.

We arrived at the town hall, outside of which I saw the most beautiful being I had yet to lay eyes on. She was a siren of few words.

Her hair long and brown was parted to each of her shoulders. Her brown eyes shined in the sun, and her smile sent shivers down my legs. Of the countless men and women that fell to my hands, none had defeated me like so.

That is how I met Callista.

Herm had to shake me three times before I would snap out of my daze.

"Ollius. Come on. We have to get inside."

"Yeah, I'm right behind you," I replied, losing track of reality.

The door shut behind us, giving way to a quiet empty room. A complete contrast of the laughter and festivities outside; the town hall was quiet and carried a serious emphasis in its silence.

"New recruit?" A deep voice rang from atop the staircase.

"The last new recruit we'll need," Herm responded.

A man of a tall figure and little to no patience rode down the staircase. His hair was golden, his eyes a dark abyss. Of all life in the cosmos, his eyes were rid of any. With every step, his aura grew more intimidating.

"You mean you actually found him?" The man asked as he approached the last few steps.

"I told you I would Thomas."

"Realistically. I had no faith in you Hermie. Good work nonetheless." Thomas praised.

Herm, now insulted, looked to me, and said,

"This is Ollius. He is a Remnant, one of the strongest I've seen in a while." Herm turned to Thomas, "I've seen what he's capable of."

"Such praise." Thomas now turned to me, "What are you capable of, Ollius?"

"Anything," I replied, crossing my arms.

Thomas smiled, turning away back up the stairs. Reaching the top of the staircase, Thomas demanded,

"Send him to the Pit. If he survives, lend him a sword against Nikolaus."

"Nikolaus? Why him?" Herm questioned.

Thomas said nothing and disappeared to the room above.

Herm stood a second before he turned a shoulder towards me. His eyes worried and his fists gripped. He grabbed my shoulder and before I knew it, we were on our way to the armory.

"Who's Nikolaus?" I asked as I followed Herm.

"A monster. Or at least that's what his enemies call him. The people here call him the Blade of the Legion. Ollius, you have to be careful." Herm warned me. "Thomas is testing you. You have to defeat Nikolaus, otherwise, we won't be able to have you here!"

I chuckled,

"I can't wait."

Arriving at the armory I saw blades and shields scattered all around, portraits of warriors on the walls, and the Spartan emblem stuck to the door. It smelled of fatigue and rotten food. Herm threw me some armor and a shield.

"Not that I need one, but do you have anything sharper than my worn-out blade?" I asked.

"We don't. I do." He replied as he withdrew his sword from his back, tossing it to me.

"Don't break it," Herm said as he dug through a chest.

"No promises."

I held a heavy blade. It was long and made of great white steel. It was a beautiful craft and Herm was a lucky man to be able to wield it. I held the long blade in one arm giving me the advantage of speed, and because of my strength—its weight.

Herm forced a smile as he tossed me a chest piece,

"Before we can worry about Nikolaus, you have to survive the Pit."

"Yeah, I still don't know what that even is."

"Probably best you don't."

We made our way to the center of the fortress, where I saw Callista, and her friends, alongside plenty of soldiers surrounding a pit dug in the ground.

"So, it's literally a pit?" I asked, turning my head to Herm.

"Well, yeah. What did you expect?" Herm answered.

"I don't know. More, I guess." I replied, staring down.

I jumped into the pit, not allowing him a sarcastic answer. I found the distance it took to reach the bottom was uncomfortably long. I underestimated how tall the walls were.

The crowd roared in excitement.

"Welcome to the Legion! We'll stop the battle if it gets too dangerous for you! Guards! Bring in the Faults!" A voice yelled among the crowds' chanting, somehow incredibly clear.

A section of the crowd disbanded, as I heard thumps of footsteps waddle towards me.

Thump. Thump. Thump.

The footsteps sang as the crowd hollered. Before long, the guard led the gigantic beast to the Pit. It was tall and gray. A truly menacing beast. Its face was twisted, its eyes the only noticeable feature as it carried only darkness. It had a figure of gluttony, and what seemed to be mud drooling out of its mouth.

It was horrifying to say the least. It easily stood eight feet tall, with gigantic teeth sharper than any blade I've yet to use.

It threw its arms to its side as it cried for blood. A wale of battle, and exhilaration.

I stared at it, as my jaw fell wide open.

I had never felt this way before. Time felt as if it stood as the beast came hurling at me. Its gigantic mud-colored arms soared through the sky, the gurgling ringing throughout my ears, my heart beating louder than its roar. My fists clenched my blade as the beast closed in. Every second invited another and every holler from the crowd only excited me.

Mere feet away, I had sprung into action.

I dashed forward, swinging my sword through its legs. As it came crumbling down, I placed my foot firmly atop the back of its head and pierced its skull. The faster I swung the blade, the brighter its glow.

Holding Herm's blade felt right. I felt at home, I felt as if I belonged. I could truly feel a different type of strength within my grasp. I couldn't explain it, but looking down on its steel, it felt warm—almost as if it didn't want me to let go.

I pulled the sword out, as I swung my arms high in victory.

"Bring me more! I demand more!" I hollered, as the crowd cheered, chanting "More!"

The crowd again disbanded, as two guards led two more beasts to my Pit.

I threw my sword behind me, as I once again dashed towards one of the beasts, tackling it down, pinning it to the ground.

I laid a barrage of fists towards its cheeks before I was pushed off by its ally. A force of undeniable strength sent me sliding across the pit.

I pulled the shield off my back as I stood up, defending one of its gigantic arms slams. I pushed its arm off, throwing my shield into its neck, it stumbled back as it held its throat.

I dodged the first beast's attack, as I climbed the second beast's arm, before jumping onto the back of the first. The beast roared as its compatriot slammed its topside in an attempt to free his friend from my grasp. It was too late however as I placed my arms thoroughly around its neck, breaking it.

The beast fell forward, I landed in front of it on my back.

The second beast hurled towards me yet again.

41

I stood up in time to grab its reaching arm, and slid in between its legs, forcing it to its back. I put my arm around its neck wrestling against its strength, connecting it with my other palm, I forced the beast into a chokehold.

I held the chokehold until I could no longer feel it fight. Its slobbering, and gurgles soon ceased. I had won the battle.

I dropped its body to my left side, as I stood up, raising one of my fists in victory.

The crowd cried, chanting my name.

Ollius! Ollius! Ollius!

Looking upon them I couldn't help but feel as if I found a home. The place I longed for my entire life. Friends, maybe even a life. I escaped the cage; I didn't want to forget that. I was free.

The cage was gone. I needed to understand this. I was no longer there.

I was no longer there.

I looked down to my palms, inside them I felt my strength pulsating. An outcry for war, for battle. I craved chaos. To a normal, sane being—this would be pandemonium, but this was all I knew. This craving was all I knew. I knew nothing of this world, nothing of these people. I knew nothing of their intentions or their strength. I just knew mine. I finally had a choice, and I refused to give it up. In that moment, looking into the crowd and feeling my strength overflow, I chose for the second time in my life: I, Ollius the Beast of Baylor, would no longer allow my voice to be stripped from me.

It was mine.

I walked towards Herm's sword, picking it up. The weight of the blade called to me. It begged me to not let go, but I knew my home was elsewhere.

I climbed the Pit, handing the sword to him.

"I didn't want to break it," I said as I patted his shoulder, making my way to the water station the Legion set up near the Pit.

Herm stood in shock. His disbelief grew by the second.

"I've never seen it do that before. It glowed."

I downed a cup of water, before turning back towards the Pit. Patiently awaiting Nikolaus.

I saw Callista stand across from me. She was on the other side of the pit, looking back at me. Her eyes, even from such a distance away, beat me to my knees. Her smile—there was something about her smile. They told stories of beauty, those eyes of an Aphrodite. I wanted to hold her, take her to faraway lands just to see her smile again. On her right ear lay a red rose, freshly picked. Her brown skin was beautiful and it invited me to get closer.

Chapter 3: Nikolaus the Blade

Shaking off my lovestruck mind, I had jumped back into the pit, awaiting Nikolaus' arrival, the crowd's cheer had died off as we all awaited a battle that was surely going to be remembered for years.

I looked at Herm, "Well? Where is this Nikolaus?"

"We sent Bryon to grab him, he should be here soon," Herm replied, crossing his arms.

"Bryon?" I asked.

"He's our resident Archer. A marksman unlike any. You'll meet him soon enough."

I grinned before I turned and pointed at a random spectator,

"You. I need your sword."

The spectator stripped his weapon, tossing me it, almost excited to be a part of the battle.

"A borrowed blade?" I heard a voice ask from beyond the crowd.

"It's a sign of respect in the Legion to return a borrowed blade, we take it very seriously here."

There was a pause before they continued, "When a warrior lends you a blade, he lends you his strength. With that comes his hopes, his responsibilities. You must Ryse."

I saw a man sneak his way through the crowd. He was short and heavy and carried a war hammer on his back. His hair was short and brown, and his eyes hazel. He was a man of age.

"Do you know what it means to Ryse, Ollius?" The man asked.

"To Ryse?"

"We Ryse not against our enemies. We Ryse amongst ourselves. We Ryse to be greater than the previous day."

"You don't have to worry about that,"

I looked back at the spectator, a young and innocent face looked back. His hair was short to a buzz, and his ears were far too big.

"I will return your sword, and I will not lose," I promised.

The kid smiled; he couldn't be older than fifteen.

I heard chatters throughout the crowd. My eyes looked for Herm, who was now standing next to the short man from before. They both gave me a nod, signaling that Nikolaus was almost here.

I grinned with excitement as a portion of the crowd disbanded yet again.

A man jumped into the Pit, he was of average build, nothing too impressive. His brown hair was short and decisive. He wore a tunic, with little to no armor. He had scars that crawled up his right arm. Yet his left arm was in pristine condition.

He walked with something to prove, almost as if he had a chip on his shoulder, weighing him down.

"You're the one everyone's been prancing about? Ollius, right?"

"Yeah, that's me. You have nothing to worry about, you'll be joining them soon enough." I replied as I pointed my borrowed blade toward him.

"Straight to the point, eh?" The man, who I assume to be Nikolaus said, as he also withdrew his sword.

"Ollius, the Beast of Baylor, they're calling you. You've got a lot to live up for with a name like that. Tell me," He paused, getting into his stance, "How did it feel slaughtering those innocent people?"

I remained quiet, gripping the blade's handle.

"I heard the tale. We all heard the tale. The tale of the Beast of Baylor. The child that just would not die." He continued, walking in circles around me.

"I'm not impressed. Strength goes beyond what's behind your swing. You're nothing but a child with a temper."

"You talk too much," I said, interrupting him.

He scoffed, "I get that a lot."

"Did you come to monologue then?"

Nikolaus scoffed yet again in response, smirking.

"No, I'm not. I'm not even here to fight you. I'm here to teach you humility. I'm here to show you the power of humanity. You took those lives, and even if they threatened yours, you still took more than you needed to."

I dashed forward swinging my sword to find a clash.

"But you really do pack a punch Ollius, you weren't kidding," Nikolaus said through strained breaths.

I forced the clash down, as I sent my left fist square through his cheek.

"Yeah, I really do," I answered as I swung my blade down.

Nikolaus dodged my swing, standing up.

"Douchebag," Nikolaus said as he swiped.

Parrying his attack, I threw my foot forward. However, before I knew it, he was behind me in an instant. I felt a grip on my thigh before I was thrown to the ground. I rolled through it, standing up. I saw a grin form on his face.

I was excited to stand against an actual competitor for I had yet to experience a true challenge. I could barely control myself. I wanted to see what Nikolaus was capable of.

Nikolaus leapt towards me.

Left. Right. Down. Right.

I blocked his attacks as they kept coming. Finding an opening, I swung my blade, Nikolaus dodged it before I tackled him to the ground, digging my blade into the floor next to us.

I grabbed his wrist, forcing his blade out. Nikolaus kicked me off him, as we both stood up.

Now both unarmed, I punched Nikolaus straight in the jaw, as he landed one of his own on my cheek. We both stumbled back. He grabbed his weapon off the ground, as I grabbed the shield from the previous battle.

I blocked his attack, before I gut-punched him with the edge, and then bashed his face with my knee. He fell back as I stood over him.

"Had enough? This doesn't have to end bloody." I warned.

"You talk too much." Nikolaus mimicked.

He stood up, this time getting in a stance.

He grabbed the tip of his blade, cutting his skin, a yellow mist enveloped his handle.

Nikolaus struck his blade on my shield, intentionally missing as I felt a slice on my right arm. I wasn't sure how he did it, but he managed to wound me.

I grabbed my arm in pain, feeling an ounce of shearing agony drip down as if a bucket overflowing.

51

Inside my arm the yellow mist stayed, exerting a throbbing sting as it dug deeper into my skin.

"Had enough? This doesn't have to end bloody."

A silence preluded, "Well, bloodier." He emphasized, chuckling.

The aching pain of my injury only enhanced my fury. I couldn't control my bloodlust. It begged me. My arms pleaded for the sweet release of my unparalleled anger. I heard a crow cry above as it soared past the Legion's walls. I felt the ground beneath me vibrate from the roars of the crowd.

None of it mattered when I felt this way. Not the crowd, not my pain, and definitely not the blood tainting the dirt I stood upon.

This is who I am.

My anger, and the chaos that chose *me*. This is who I was destined to be.

This was *my* story. No one would dare write it for me.

I shouted, breaking the handle to the shield I was holding.

Nikolaus gripped his blade close, preparing to anticipate my attack.

As if he could defend against *my* power.

I sent my fist towards his blade, shattering it into two. I grabbed Nikolaus by his neck, slamming him down to the ground. I looked into his eyes as I held his life in my hands. He stared back at me, fearless. Even in the face of death, the uncertainty of the extent of a stranger's wrath, Nikolaus never lost his grin.

At that moment I stared into his soul, I saw his past, his future, his present. I saw loved ones, I saw potential. I wanted to take it from him. His life, his friends, his future. At that moment, I felt my rage win. My eyes lit up, my heart cried, and my mind raced with the tortuous possibilities I could put him through.

But I let him go.

Against every fiber of my being begging me to fight. Against every thought of merciless slaughter, I let him go.

There's an instinct in all of us to stay alive; to stay in control. It's a difficult thing to comprehend, but it's there—the sixth sense of control. For most of our lives, we'll take it for granted. For we think our actions are our own yet fail to realize how heavily influenced they truly are. From the ale we sip to the people we call friends; we are never in control.

The crowd cheered as I walked away from Nikolaus, although exhausted and out of breath. I heard men and women chanting my name and I couldn't help but think this was where I belonged.

I looked at Callista. Her blush was the strongest hit I took that day.

Chapter 4: The First of Many

Shortly after the battle with Nikolaus, Herm and I met with Thomas. He was pleased to say the least. Moreover, he was shocked that Nikolaus could lose to anyone. He wasted no time appointing me to the 5th Circle.

The Legion was built up of 7 Circles. Essentially, a Circle was a guild of sorts. They handled missions and different types of assignments. As a member of the 5th Circle, I roomed with Hermaeus, Stergious, the short man from before, Daniil, Bryon, and Nikolina. Three of whom I have yet to meet.

The next day, Herm introduced me to different members of the Legion. We spent the morning talking and I got to know my other roommates. Daniil was essentially the pushover of the group. He handled the odd jobs that nobody else wanted to do. Moreover, Daniil was reliable.

Bryon was the archer of the group—and according to Herm, he was the best at camp. His eyes could see miles away. Realistically, the only reason I think he trained for archery is because he was too lazy for battle. He would do what needs to be done, nothing more, usually less.

Nikolina was Nikolaus' twin. I could tell before I was told. She had long brown hair as opposed to his short brown hair. Their brown eyes shared the same egotistical prowess. Not to mention, their simper. The only difference I could see between the two was that Nikolina wore glasses, and she was not a warrior. According to Hermaeus, she was the strategist of the Circle. Every Circle had one, it was mandatory. Essentially, they were trained to handle different situations and to come up with plans when needed. They weren't leaders, just the ones to turn to when the mission takes a turn for the worst.

Later in the evening, the 5th Circle was called to the town hall. Apparently, before I had even arrived, Thomas had been preparing for the fight back. They certainly had the resources and the men for a proper assault, and for that reason, I was confused as to why they had not yet done so.

We sat in a room with a table planted in the middle. Curtains were blocking the outside from seeing in, which led me to believe that this was top secret. At the table sat Herm, Stergious, Bryon,

Nikolina, Daniil, and I. At the far end of the table, next to a board of sorts stood Thomas.

"Members of the Fifth. Tonight, we take the first step towards the revival of Sparta. Within the next month, Epaminondas will fall to our hands." Thomas said, standing over the round table we were all summoned to.

"Wait, Matullus found it?" Herm asked with either shock or excitement in his voice.

"It wasn't easy. But Matullus managed to pinpoint a location, though not precise." Thomas responded.

"I hope you don't expect us to spend years looking through an entire continent for an artifact," Stergious responded.

"You'll do as you're told Sterg. But no, it's not that vast. It's located on a small island, west of the coast of Kavala. With magic like the one protecting the artifact, this is the closest Matullus can get." Thomas replied, sternly.

"An entire island?" Bryon responded.

He continued, "There's got to be a better way."

"This is the only way." Thomas snapped.

"We've spent years looking for the Gem! We finally have a lead, and you're complaining!? For the first time in eighteen years, we have a shot!" He continued.

"Simmer down, Thomas." I interrupted.

"You pledged your lives for the revival of Sparta. If something's changed, speak up now." Thomas lectured.

"Daniil and I have yet to say a word, Thomas," Nikolina said, breaking the tension.

"You leave when dawn breaks. Get some rest, I'll have preparations ready. The Sixth Circle will be joining you." Thomas said as he turned away from the table.

"You find the artifact and bring it back to camp safely. That is your mission. Sterg is in charge, Herm is second. Report to me, and me alone when you get back." Thomas continued.

"Ryse!" The group yelled as they broke.

"Ollius. I need you to stay behind." Thomas said as he turned around.

The group dispersed, as I stood up walking toward Thomas.

"Yeah?" I asked.

"Your priorities, Ollius. I need to know where they're at." He said, not turning back towards me.

"I don't know. As far as it stands now, the Legion is all I've got. I don't have a family; I don't have friends." I answered.

"That's not good enough—"

"It doesn't have to be."

"You don't understand. It won't be like this forever. The Legion is standing strong right now, true. However—there is always a tide Ollius. We need to make a move before it's too late. You're strong. I need you on our side." There was a pause before he continued, turning his head towards me, his dark black eyes emphasizing his appellation as the leader of the Legion, "I need you to come back with the Gem, more than anything. I want you to promise me you will."

"I promise you. The next time you'll see me, it'll be with the Gem."

Thomas broke a smile, before turning away yet again.

I caught Herm as we all headed back to our barracks.

"It's about time I finally see you in battle, Herm," I said as I walked alongside him towards the bridge.

Herm smiled, "I'll have you going in circles, Ollius."

I smirked, "See you tomorrow."

The rest of the night was quiet. I crashed in my bed as my mind raced for hours. I wasn't afraid, and I was incapable of doubting myself. However, I felt worried, nonetheless. Not for me, but for my brothers in arms. Over the next couple of days, we'll be facing all types of foes. I can handle myself, but I was not so sure of my teammates. This was a new feeling for me. I had never experienced worry for someone else. I felt weak and vulnerable.

I awoke at the break of dawn. Sunlight broke through the window to my left to fill in my empty room. I hated being alone. After spending so much of my life in isolation, being alone was arduous. It reminded me of the pain I had to endure during my imprisonment. Moreover, it reminded me that at one time, I was held, hostage. It angered me when I realized how powerless I was before that child released me.

That's when it hit me. There was something crawling in my head. I couldn't pinpoint it, but I knew there was something wrong. I was uncomfortable, and I couldn't figure out why.

A knock on the door woke me from my daze. I stood from my bed and opened it to see Daniil standing at my door. Daniil was a good kid. He was reliable and quick on his feet. He was a little shorter than average and had gray eyes that reminded me of a cloudy day. However, he was incredibly annoying.

"Hey, Ollius. You awake?" Daniil asked as he looked into my eyes.

"What do you think?" I responded.

"Well, I was just asking."

"What do you need?" I replied, my voice defeated.

"Well, Thomas sent me to wake everyone up. He wanted me to give you a message."

A silence took over the conversation.

"Well? What did he want me to know?" I asked, a little annoyed.

"He wanted me to tell you to wake up and get ready."

"You realize you could've just told me this at the beginning of the conversation, right? We didn't need to have this painful interchange." I asked as I planted my face inside my palm.

"Well. Now you know." Daniil said as he walked away.

I closed the door and got ready for the adventure. I packed some of the food I had inside the backpack the Legion provided me. I grabbed my blade, sheathing it. It was the only possession I had, truthfully. A blade, taken from Vassilios; the man responsible for Dimitris' murder. I grabbed a shield I got from Sterg and holstered it on my back. I had provisions, water, and other essentials packed and headed out to meet Herm at the start of the bridge.

The walk to the bridge wasn't long. I spent most of it examining my equipment, and double-checking that I had everything ready for a trip.

"You ready?" I asked as I approached Hermaeus.

"As ready as I can be. We're having Daniil carry all the provisions, so I've been up all-night packing with him." He replied.

"Where's the rest of our Circle?" I asked, looking around.

"Probably all depositing before leaving for the trip," Herm replied, looking down with his arms crossed.

"Depositing? Depositing what?"

"Before every trip, every member of a Circle is required to deposit a drop of blood at the Temple of Ares." He replied, raising his head to meet my eyes.

"What? I wasn't told about this." I replied, throwing my arms up in confusion.

"Really? It's not too late for you to make it to the Temple. It's just down next to the entrance."

I took my first steps toward the Temple. It's a little weird to be giving out just a single drop of my blood, but if it meant being a part of a group dynamic for the first time in my life, it'd be worth the effort. I crossed the bridge and took a right towards the entrance of the Legions camp. It took me some time to find, but eventually, I found the Temple of Ares. It was a white building, carried by pillars. I took a step inside to find a red-orange atmosphere. The light of the torches heated up the inside of the Temple. Almost as soon as I stepped inside, I started sweating. This place was a furnace. There were structures, all types of different weapons, and other memorabilia of Ares strung up on the walls.

Weirdly. I felt a sense of belonging here. It was almost as if this was where I was meant to be. Maybe it was because of my Spartan blood, or my ache for battle but I didn't want to leave.

"Warrior. I assume you're here to deposit." A soft-spoken woman spoke from across the Temple, interrupting my train of thought, I turned around.

"Yeah. I'm a Warrior from the Fifth Circle. We're setting out on a mission today; I was told I'd have to give up a drop of blood." I replied.

"This way, Warrior. Your teammates are already here." She replied, leading the way downstairs.

I followed her, a little weary of what I'd have to do. We arrived downstairs, where I saw the other members of the Fifth Circle around a table with all types of equipment on it.

"You finally showed up," Sterg said from behind me.

"It's your turn," Nikolina said, a cold tone enveloping her tongue.

"What do you need me to do?" I asked as I approached the table.

"Take this, pinch your fingertip, and allow the drop of blood to drop into this canister here." The soft-spoken woman instructed, handing me a tiny needle.

I went to pinch my fingertip, just for the needle to snap.

"I think I'm going to need something a lot stronger than this," I said, as I handed the broken needle to the soft-spoken woman.

For the next few minutes, we tried multiple needles, even took to blades, but none could penetrate my skin. This was a strange phenomenon, as I have been hurt before. I had bled in the battle with Nikolaus not long ago, so I was puzzled as to why I couldn't hurt myself.

"I got it, just take a drop from me, we have to get going," Sterg said, offering his arm.

The woman took another drop of Sterg's blood, and we called it a day. We all headed back up to the bridge where Herm and the Sixth Circle were awaiting our arrival. Herm was leaning over the bridge, as the entire Sixth Circle surrounded him talking and laughing. From the Sixth Circle, I only recognized one, Nikolaus of the Blade.

"Took you guys long enough." Nikolaus said, greeting us.

"Well, we're here now," Sterg replied.

"We're running a little behind, let's hurry it up." A short member of the Sixth Circle I have yet to meet said.

"We'll be headed west of camp, towards Mare Forest. Through there, we have a Remnant waiting at the bay of the Coast of Kavala, who will take us to the island." The short skinny member of the Sixth Circle continued. He wore glasses and a fearful smile. His clothes were built of a soft brown cloth.

"Mare Forest?" I asked.

"It's a large forest, said to be filled to the brim with supernatural creatures. Nothing we can't handle." Nikolaus answered.

"Don't worry. We got your back Ollius." Herm announced.

"I'm Aristos, the strategist of the Sixth Circle. This is Ochos, our resident archer. You've obviously met Nikolaus, and finally, Cilla of the Helm."

"Nice to meet you guys. I'm Ollius of the Fifth. We should get going, truly." I responded, excited to get started on my first adventure.

The 5th Circle and the 6th Circle were some of the strongest that inhabited the Legion. Although there were still some incredible talents among the other Circles, ones that rivaled even Nikolaus.

We walked for hours before we reached the forest. I passed trees, people, and animals of varying sizes. I truly got to see some incredible beauty.

Though, none that remotely reminded me of Callista's smile.

The 6th Circle was kind. Although Ochos and Cilla didn't say much. I did get along with Aristos and Nikolaus. Even after the battle we just had, Nikolaus accepted me as one of his own. I felt an immediate connection with him. Hermaeus was still my favorite to talk to as he always knew how to make me, and everyone else laugh. I enjoyed his company. Sterg told us stories about his adventures before the Legion with Sparta's armies. They fought off incredible creatures to keep their home safe. I was almost jealous of not having any stories I could return the favor with.

Chapter 5: The Mare Forest

Approaching the forest, I felt a sense of danger. It was dark and ominous. The night sky was getting prominent as we finally found a place to settle in for the night. Aristos set up a campfire as everyone chatted around it. Herm and Nikolina were off from the group having their own private conversation. Aristos and Nikolaus were hanging out while cooking up some food. Sterg was lecturing Daniil in the corner of our camp, while I sat back and stared at the night sky. So many stars, so many stories. I craved to learn them, more importantly, I craved to create some of my own.

I felt an unfamiliar relationship with the stars. They felt magical, and they fascinated me beyond belief. The stories they told were rare and known around the world.

When would it be my turn?

Eventually, we all dozed off in preparation for the morning's adventures.

Sometime throughout the night, I was awoken from my slumber by a faraway scream. Someone was in danger. I rose to my feet, looking at the other members. They were all fast asleep beside Daniil. Before I could try to wake someone up, Daniil dashed past me with a speed I didn't think he was capable of.

"Daniil! Come back! It's dangerous!" I shouted before I followed. We ran towards the scream for a few minutes before I finally stopped him.

"Don't run off like that. Something doesn't feel right here." I lectured as I looked around us. Nothing but foliage and trees. There were absolutely no signs of life. No crickets, no buzzing, no sounds of sticks breaking—nothing. The forest was entirely silent.

"Do you know the way back to camp?" I asked as I looked around us.

"No. I just kind of started running. Someone was screaming!" He answered.

"Keep it down!" I shouted back.

"We don't know who or what's out here. We're the ones in danger. We have to find a way out of the forest." I replied, turning away.

"But what about the others? If we're in danger, they are too." Daniil said.

"Not necessarily. Look around you. There is absolutely nothing around us. Don't you think it's odd we were the only two awoken by the sound? When I shouted after you, no one woke up to help us. The fact that we're the only ones awake right now in this entire forest, means we're the prey." I said as I withdrew my sword.

I could hear Daniil gulp.

"Come on. If we keep going in one direction, eventually, we'll hit the edge of the forest." I lead the way, paving a path with my blade.

Suddenly, behind us, we heard a siren of sorts. It was a song. A very eerie song to hear in the middle of the night in a dark forest. The creature was harmonizing.

Hmmm… Hmmm… Hmmm…

Daniil started freaking out, pulling on his dark and messy, unkempt hair.

"Calm down. We know where it is now, we'll just go the other way. It's fine, we have to believe we're faster than it." I said, trying to calm him down.

Daniil took off the other way, I followed with my sword to my side.

Suddenly, we heard another siren in the direction we were running, Daniil took a hard left running with all his might. Before long, another siren sang in that same direction, and when we took a hard turn, there was another. We were surrounded in all four directions.

Daniil fell to his knees, defeated. The sirens were closing in.

"Come on, we can't give up. We have to keep fighting. We will make it out of this forest tonight." I said, trying to build up any hope that was left.

"Listen to their song Ollius! The distance between them is always the same! No matter how close one gets, the other three follow! There's nothing we can do! No matter where we run, they follow. They just know! Which means we can't hide!" Daniil screamed; his eyes, although a light gray, were rid of any color.

"So what?! What does sitting here and crying do for us? We are warriors! We run, and if they catch up to us, we fight! If you can't win, don't worry— because I can!" I grabbed him and threw him on my shoulder as I dashed towards the center of two sirens. I can outrun them; I just know I can.

My feet shot through plants and breezed past trees. I jumped over rocks, fallen logs, and animals long lost in the dream realm.

For what felt like hours I kept running, and the sirens kept the same distance away from me, slowly closing in. The forest was endless, but so was my stamina. I refused to give up, and I only felt my speed increase as the hopelessness of the situation only became clearer. I ran, and I ran, but the sirens were just as fast.

Eventually, they were only a couple of feet away in all four directions.

I collapsed, dropping Daniil.

We stood up in haste. I withdrew my sword, preparing myself for battle.

Daniil stood up, standing back-to-back with me, as he removed his dagger from his boot.

As we waited for death to close in, I could hear Daniil's heart beat louder than the Sirens.

I heard Daniil shout a scream of horror; I turned around, before suddenly I found myself awake in the exact spot I had fallen asleep in. My clothes were drenched with sweat and I disregarded that as I rose to look for Daniil. He had just woken up on the other side of the camp and looked to be sweating as well. He had a deep bruise on the left side of his neck that took attention away from his buzzed haircut.

He looked away in shame the moment our eyes locked.

He was quiet and refused to talk about what he saw for the rest of the day. I agreed not to tell everyone, for Daniil did not want to relive what he experienced that night. We walked till the sun gave out, and then some.

During the trip out of the forest, I couldn't help but feel a bit of anxiety dance around me. Daniil would not survive another night here, we had to get out as fast as we could. The warriors had no idea of the creatures that haunted this accursed forest.

So we spent hours listening to Sterg's stories, one that stood out especially was his victory over a dragon.

It wasn't before it was late at night before we finally broke free of the Mare Forest. I saw a weight climb off Daniil's shoulders—before another climbed atop. He took an abrupt stop and frantically looked in all directions.

"You guys hear that right?" He exclaimed as he removed his dagger from his boot.

We all looked at each other in confusion.

"Put down your blade," Nikolaus said as he held his sheathed.

The other members of the 6th Circle followed suit.

"Blades away. Let's all calm down." Nikolina said, trying to put a stop to what would be an ugly situation.

"There's someone laughing all around us. Can't you guys hear them?!" Daniil said, objectively freaking out.

"I said, put down your blade Daniil. Let's calm down." Nikolaus said, raising his arms toward him.

"But the laughing Nikolaus, do you not hear it?!" Daniil hollered.

"Daniil. You're the only one hearing it. Calm down. We can protect you. Remember your training." Nikolaus replied, as he took yet another step toward him.

Daniil stuck his gaze to Nikolaus and eventually grew enough strength to drop his dagger.

Daniil looked down, and threw his hands to his ears, trying to block out the laughter.

"I need to tell you guys something," I spoke up as I walked toward Daniil.

"Last night. We were preyed on by a spirit of the Mare Forest." I continued.

Multiple questions arose from the group all built around one, "Why didn't you tell us?"

"I wasn't at liberty to say until it became a danger to the group. Daniil was the only one affected. I didn't want to take that choice from him." I answered, as I put my arm on Daniil's back, trying to comfort him.

"It was late at night when it happened. Sirens arose from all around us, and we were forced to run for hours. I ran till they caught up with me—there was nothing else I could do. They sang and sang all around us. Daniil and I picked up our blades, but before I could swing one, we awoke back at camp, with the mysterious bruise on his neck." I explained, as the group listened with their ears perked.

"Sirens that loud? How did we not hear them?" Nikolina asked.

"Nothing in the forest was awake. The animals, the insects, I think even the trees were asleep. There was not an ounce of life in that forest beside Daniil's and mine. They preyed on us. I don't know why I wasn't affected. I guess they were after Daniil from the beginning." I replied.

"Whatever the reason was. Daniil is suffering. We have to get him treatment. That is our top priority." Nikolaus said, looking back at Daniil, who had now fallen to his knees.

"Our top priority is the mission, Nikolaus." Ochos, their archer, replied.

"Finally decided to speak up, Ochos?" I asked, crossing my arms.

"We must complete this mission. One man's life is not worth the future of Sparta. This is our chance." Ochos replied, meeting his gaze with mine.

Brave man.

"For a man of few words, you still managed to find the exact ones to piss me off," I said as I took a step towards him. Nikolaus sprung into action, holding me back.

"Sparta fell for one reason. It's not that we were weaker, or slower, or dumber than our enemy.

It's because we left behind our brothers! We let them die because we believed—let me go, Nikolaus!" I lectured as I tossed Nikolaus to the side. His body flew into a pile of mud nearby.

"If we keep the same mindset of leaving behind our brothers in arms, we will never win! He'd kill for you; he'd die for you!" I hollered as I sent a fist across Ochos' face.

Ochos flew and fell on his back in a pile of mud.

"Don't ever talk about one of us like that again. I promise I won't give you another chance." I said as I turned around to grab Daniil.

"Wait! Nikolina and Bryon can take Daniil back to camp. We'll continue the mission." Sterg demanded. I took a second before letting go of Daniil. In the time we spent together, I truly learned why the Legion was lucky to have him.

He was innocent. He wasn't the strongest soldier, true, or even the most reliable. But he had one thing we all lacked—compassion.

"You act as if you're in charge, Beast," Ochos said through gritted teeth.

"I promised Thomas the Gem, I never promised him your safety Ochos." I paused, before continuing.

Chapter 6: Dawn

The group continued. It was just me, Herm, Sterg, and the other members of the 6th Circle. Whatever was ahead of us next, I was more than prepared to handle. Call it anger, call it fury, it didn't matter. I needed something, or someone to punch. Seeing Daniil on his knees like that angered something inside me. It called for a forgotten bicker for battle. Life was usually unfair like that for whether it was a pit or a battle for your very spirit, we were all fighting our demons. Life would be meaningless if not for the struggle between man and self. Without a battle, we'd live our life seamlessly, day in and day out, carefree.

Some take on the pain of others, and some simply ignore their own—but at the end of the day, the battle carries on.

Trouble didn't take long to find its way into our midst, as only half a day after we left the Forest, we came up against a mysterious man in black before night broke. The skies, a healthy orange, as a purple haze found itself riding its outskirts. A battalion of stars caught the spotlight of the coral moon crest that remarked a beautiful twilight. He stood in the middle of a field, staring at us. I stopped the group, confused as to what he was doing. I felt a sort of presence from that man. It was sinister and otherworldly. Within the silk fabric of the black robe rode the eerie threads of a sinister design.

I whistled, as I broke away from the road.

The men of the Legion followed me, as Aristos grabbed Ochos' shoulder, signaling him to stay behind.

"Take it easy. He could be innocent." Sterg warned.

"I don't care." I replied, gripping the handle to the worn-out steel I wielded proudly.

It didn't take us long to reach the hooded man. There was just something about him that I didn't like. I didn't know if it was his smell or his stance. Maybe the way his robe was perched over his head, or the aura that escaped from his threads.

Maybe it was all of it.

He wasn't far, but we took our time. I ordered the group to surround him as soon as we got there.

"Can we help you?" I asked, as we closed in.

"There's nothing you could do for me, Spartan—nor would you want to." He replied, his voice deep, dominant, and heavy.

"Spartan? What do you know about Sparta?" I asked, as we surrounded him, circling slowly.

"More than you're comfortable with, Ollius." He said, raising his head.

There was a split second where I caught a glimpse of his eyes. And in that moment, I felt true fear for the first time in my life. The type of fear that would have you questioning life, and if it was worth living. For if there was such a thing as true evil, then true good was not on your side. The type of fear to put doubt in peace and sanctuary, tainting the very ground you stand upon. Trust becomes a deceiving usurper; good is lost to time. There was no life in those eyes. There was no good, no hope. Only a story of endless slaughter and a craving for chaos—unapologetic chaos. The man that stood before me was evil incarnate, evil if it could walk, sit, breathe, eat, sleep. Eyes so red, they could only be described as an ocean of blood just waiting to swallow the beholder. For a second there, I forgot about the fact that he knew my name—my thoughts were empty. I only felt the raging rumbling for escape. The ocean of blood was nearing me every moment that passed. Calling to me, as if it was a bid for a voyage.

Inside my chest, I felt a chilly glacier invade. I felt cold and weak. My arms shook; my hands felt useless against the man that stood mere feet in front of me; my blade, dull; my head, loud. A threatening aura—a killer—a primal instinct, I couldn't find the words to describe the aura I felt rummage through his embers. I felt true evil, and any action or word I could take towards him was futile. There was not a thing I could do to stop him, for there was no mercy within those cold, red eyes. If someone like him could exist— then the Gods have truly forgotten us.

"All of you. Head back." I ordered.

Almost as if in unison, I felt their eyes shoot toward me. A wave of confusion and frustration lingered in the air around us.

"What's wrong?" Sterg reached out, his curiosity went unanswered. A desperate thirst, unquenched.

"I'm not asking you, Sterg. Trust me—all of you, get back to the road." I ordered, with a tone more demanding than the previous.

It took a second, but it wasn't long before they decided to trust me. The team dispersed, heading back towards the road, alongside murmurs of hesitancy.

"Fear? It's a good look on you." The man replied, his voice a dagger, stuck to the deepest parts of my soul. A familiar voice yet forgotten. I felt a spiral of freezing cold drive towards my knees.

"Don't flatter yourself." I replied, confused; as my arm bid for battle, my gut yearned for escape. My intuition was screaming at me to run. Fear called out to me as a trench of unease and worry slowly dug itself within my chest, ridding me of any confidence, of any hope.

I heard a chuckle coming from underneath his hood.

"You can run, just not anywhere that I can't catch you. You can hide, just not anywhere that I can't find you. You can scream, Son of Sparta. Just not to anyone that can help you. I am the inevitable, I am the impossible." I heard a thunderclap in the distance as gray clouds rolled into view, "Look at your friends, Ollius."

I shot my eye to my side as a dark gray haze rode towards them from above.

"In an instant, I could take their lives—and you know I can." The mysterious man threatened. I looked back with uncertainty in my eyes. For the first time in my life, I didn't know what I wanted to do.

"The fear in your eyes; it's beautiful."

"What do you want?" I asked, my voice defeated.

The man chuckled,

"To see you lose everything."

I took a second before responding, "That's not happening."

"It already is, Ollius. I am going to ruin you."
The mysterious man replied, his voice louder, charged
with emphasis, as he closed in on me at a blinding
speed.

"I'd rather suffer a thousand deaths before I bow
down to another man."

"You will suffer a thousand deaths, Son of
Sparta. However—none of them will be yours. I will
take everyone you love, Ollius."

"I'll kill you before you ever get the chance, you
freak," I announced as I took a step away.

"Your father said the same thing. That's why
I'm standing here, and he isn't."

I let my blade free of its sheath, and a moment
later I found it inside the man's gut, staining it red.

"You really thought that would be enough?"
The robe lifted, revealing a grin of overconfidence.

"I'll be seeing you around." A voice said,
behind me.

I shot around, blade at the ready, to see nothing. He was gone in a flash. My companions made their way to me hastily to see nothing but an empty field, and a dark robe on the ground below.

"Did you kill him? Where'd he go?" Herm asked.

"No. I didn't. I'm not sure how—I saw him bleed!"

"Take the robe, we can have Matullus take a look at it back at camp," Sterg ordered as Herm followed his demand.

"Let's go." I ordered, visibly frustrated I walked back towards the road.

"Hold up Ollius, what'd he say to you?" Herm peered.

"It doesn't matter." I replied looking back at him.

"He mentioned your father." Sterg chimed in, "I heard him say it."

"You have no right to mention my father!" My eyes glimmered with a fit of indescribable anger, as I drove my face towards Sterg, closing the distance between us in a moment. Sterg didn't reply; he and Herm continued onto the road, as I followed shortly after. Cilla followed me, quietly observing. She's been quiet the whole trip. She stood at a light five foot eight and was honestly a little pretty. Her hair short and black, and her eyes a beautiful shade of green.

"You're angry." Her voice rang through my ears. It was my first time hearing her speak.

"I might be." I replied, as she caught up to my speed, walking next to me along the path laid ahead of us.

"It's okay to be angry. I'm always angry." She said, looking down.

There was a silence before I spoke,

"Good for you."

"My father was King Agesilaus. The Helm was mine, ya know?"

The silence returned before I continued,

"Good for you." I emphasized.

She broke half a smile. Something I don't think anyone's ever seen before.

I didn't have any patience left for her.

I didn't care much in that moment. I only felt my rage brew. Bubbling, and overwhelming the brim of its bucket.

We spent the rest of the day walking toward Kavala. It was definitely quite a distance away. I spent that time recalling how I got to this very moment. I found freedom, and it was bittersweet. I could do anything I wanted to, go anywhere I wanted to go. Only a week ago, I was still rotting in that cage. Today, I walked alongside talented warriors, set on a mission to remind Greece of the shadow in its midst. At that moment, I wanted to bring Sparta back more than ever. Not because I cared about some nationalism ideology. I just wanted to fight against my prison, my cage, the man in the robe—I wanted to escape. As simple as that sounds, I couldn't help but feel the way

I did. Rageful, yet empty. I wanted a purpose past what my fists ached for. I finally had the chance to, through bringing Sparta back. Dimitris' screams still haunted me. I wasn't strong enough to save him, and that weighed heavily on me. I dug in my backpack to grab a piece of cloth. When I left Mizeria, in between the adrenaline, the heavy rain, and the blood of my enemies, I managed to pick up the piece of cloth he wore around his neck. It was red and made up of very expensive material. It was the only keepsake I had of him. I carried it with me to remind myself that I was never alone. The sunlight I appreciate now could not have been possible if it wasn't for Dimitris.

Chapter 7: The City of Kavala

One especially hot afternoon, we finally stepped foot in Kavala. It was a gigantic core of mud-brick homes and a river that shot through the middle of the city. The homes carried a tent on top to block out the blazing sun. Each home had the same beige color and a brown wooden door. It was a city of poverty.

Aristos had an idea for hiding my face, one that I hated. My eyes were a dead giveaway of who I was, and we couldn't afford to deal with that problem.

Herm dug inside his pack to bring out the dark robe from before.

"I'm not wearing that." I said, shaking my head.

"Yes, you are. We have nothing else, and no time to find you something else." Sterg said.

"We'll make do. I doubt they'll be able to recognize me to begin with." I argued.

"Put the robe on. It's just until we've cleared Kavala. This is a major city; they've heard stories of the Beast of Baylor and we can't afford for you to get caught. It shouldn't take more than a day." Aristos pressured.

"Fine. You all better pick up the pace though." I said as I grabbed the robe, throwing it over my head.

We made our way down the hill, following the path ahead of us. Kavala held a sense of beauty in its less-than-appealing architecture. I could sense the atmosphere before me. It was welcoming and offered an embrace to any visitor to step inside.

We continued the path ahead of us, eventually finding a market, one with groceries, clothing, and other necessities. As we passed by, my eyes followed a beautiful tunic that laid just a few feet away from me. I stopped, as the rest of the Legion continued to go on, oblivious to the fact that I had just parted away from the group.

"Caught your eye, huh?" The acquisitive trader said. His mustache was soaked with sweat.

"Yeah. It's beautiful. How much?" I asked, my head lowered.

"Twenty Reels for the right customer." The man answered, his voice eager for my coins.

That's when I came upon the realization that I do not have said coins.

"Actually. I'm not interested. Thank you." I said as I looked up, trying to see how the man looked so I could return at a later time. The clouds blocked the sun as I shot my eyes toward him.

That was my first mistake.

The man fell back in complete horror. His face, a petrifying ache of fear. Every muscle in his body froze as his eyes grew cold.

"Your eyes!" The man stuttered before continuing, "They're glowing! Your eyes are glowing red!" The man crawled backwards hitting the stall behind him. He grabbed the back of his head in pain as he continued, "You're him! The Beast of Baylor!" His voice cracked. From the deepest trenches of this man's soul rose terror of the highest caliber, a shout of unease and dread, a holler of fear. His friends, family, neighbors, and customers were all in danger. Standing before him was a monster of strength and a patriot of death. "You're real! Somebody call the guards!" The man shouted, climbing to his feet, hoping to flee away from the beast standing mere feet away.

Before I knew it, I was surrounded yet again by guards with bronze swords. They shouted, demanding I tear off my hood.

I was faced with a horrible choice; to submit to these lowly beings and stoop to their level, risking the mission, or offering myself up so my comrades might escape. The thought of being trapped yet again angered me.

Looking into the guards' eyes, I saw beyond their commands. In their eyes I saw families, I saw loved ones, I saw a future, and more importantly a past.

I chose the latter, revealing my face as I tore off my hood.

My eyes lit a crimson red as the guards and citizens surrounding me gasped in horror.

"Beast of Baylor! Under the power and land of King Illunus, I arrest you for the massacre of the victims of Mizeria." A guard spoke as they closed in on me, arresting me.

Within the next hour, I was taken to the center of town in a jail surrounded by walls taller than that of the Legions. It was modest. At least this time around I had sunlight, and people to talk to. Nonetheless, my mind thought back to the trapdoor. The guards surrounded the common area past the bars. Inside stood the hardened criminals of Kavala. I had no plans to sit around for years in this hole—I would make my escape come nightfall.

I stared up towards the ceiling of the jail as I laid on the ground below, patiently awaiting the night before I was interrupted by a voice across from me.

"Do you really need an extra helping of bread, Ghastodos?" A man said.

"What did you say to me?" A deep voice replied.

"Couldn't hear me pass your belly, Babis?" The man replied, as I heard a scuffle and then a holler.

"That'll teach you to be greedy." The man said as I heard footsteps follow towards me.

"New guy. Heads up, I got a present for you."

"Not interested. Leave me alone." I replied, my head still staring at the ceiling, resting on my hands.

"Suit yourself." I heard a crunch before he continued, "Some of the other inmates told me you're who they call the Beast of Baylor. I heard your tale. Although I'm not sure I believe it."

"I honestly do not care. Go bother someone else." I replied.

"I could. I'd just rather bother you." He paused, before continuing, "I'm Triton. My friends call me Tri."

I finally turned my head towards the man.

"What do you want, Triton?" I asked.

"A way out. If the tales are true, you're quite a strong man. Maybe we could work together." Triton had long blond hair that was bundled up in a ponytail.

His eyes an ocean blue, and his smile radiant. He stood tall, and carried muscles, although he had a slender physique.

"I might be inclined to. What's in it for me?" I asked, sitting up.

"A friend?" He offered.

I scoffed, "Alright. My name's Ollius." I offered my hand.

He shook it, and we spent the rest of the day talking. He was an orphan that knew nothing about his parents. The only companion he had growing up was a blade that could only be wielded by him. He wouldn't go into specifics, but it was special to him. I related to him as I too had no idea of who my parents were and grew up with nobody but Demetris. He was a thief, forced to steal for his own survival. That was the reason he was in jail.

I found that I could also relate to his criminal past and let out a chuckle when he mentioned it.

"Tonight. We'll make a break for it, Triton. I can take you to your blade, but after, we must part ways." I said, extending my arm.

"That works for me, Ollius. Pray the Gods our paths cross once again." Triton replied, shaking it. I was shocked as we grew to be good friends in a short time. I felt connected to Triton, it was a connection I couldn't figure out.

Later on, that night, Triton and I found ourselves arguing over the plan.

"Triton. I'm telling you; our best bet is to scale the wall! If we shred the wall to pieces, the other dangerous convicts will escape too!" I hollered.

"Come on! They're not that bad once you get to know them!" Triton screamed back.

"Out of the question!" I emphasized, "You think I can't tear down a wall—that's what you're insinuating! Have you seen me?" I yelled even louder, replying to his hysterics.

"Yes, I have! That's the problem! I think you're too weak and too scared to handle releasing a bunch of convicts—"

I punched Triton, sending him into the ground below, interrupting his sentence.

"You said something about being too weak? You coward!" I shouted, staring him down, my eyes enveloping the same crimson aura from before.

Triton tackled me to the ground, almost unexpectedly. We fought on the ground for a bit, as a guard shouted for us to stop.

"I'll kill you where you stand! Let go of him now Beast!" The guard shouted as he unlocked the cage and dashed towards us.

I grabbed the guard by the collar, throwing him towards me as I kneed his stomach knocking the wind clean out of him.

I grabbed the keys that were latched onto his belt as I helped Triton up.

"Come on. We're short on time." I said as I made my way to the door.

I reached the gate, unlocking it, clearing a path for me and Triton to escape. I slammed the door behind me, locking it, staring into the eyes of a fellow convict, I found myself smirking.

We took a stroll down the hallway, knocking out every guard in our way. Triton punched a guard in my direction so I could send another one to his other cheek, putting him to sleep. We had some fun fighting together and found each other to be compatible fighters. Our fighting styles differed, but we both packed a punch capable of dazing a trained soldier. His fighting style was smoother, it involved a lot of grappling, as mine mostly depended on the speed and the power behind my swing.

The time came when we reached the wall at the end of the cells. I sent a fist towards the mud-brick wall, tearing a hole as if it were cardboard. I climbed through as Triton did the same. We walked across the grass enclosure as we reached a gigantic wall that stood between us and freedom.

"You're definitely strong, but how fast are you?" Triton challenged.

I smirked, "If you need help climbing down, I'll be ready to catch you." I replied, reaching for the wall.

Not long after I beat Triton down the wall, we made our way to the Town Hall, where I helped Triton take back his blade. When we first arrived at the Town Hall, we got some information out of the entrance guards about where its location is. Apparently, it was gifted to some knight with royal heritage—just some spoiled kid with too much time on his hands. We walked into the barracks where the blade sent itself towards Triton as soon as he walked into the room. It had a personality and a mind of its own. A truly magnificent piece, built for a warrior. Its steel was strong and looked to be new. The hilt of the blade was shaped like a Hammerhead shark and was built of a beautiful shade of light blue metal, the pommel the same.

After we took back the blade, we met outside to say our goodbyes.

"Thanks for all you've done for me. Get back to your crew safely."

I shook his hand, leading him into a hug, "I'm sure our paths will cross once again."

I turned around, walking towards the Coast of Kavala before I heard Triton shout,

"Hey, that punch of yours hurt, it didn't feel like you held back."

"That's because I didn't." I turned my head, winking.

I was making my way towards the coast before a guard from the prison revealed himself to me.

"Beast! You're not going anywhere—"

The guard was interrupted by the flat side of Hermaeus' sword. He fell forward, dropping his weapon and shield to the side.

"Hermaeus!" I greeted excitedly, my arms open.

"Quiet down. What happened anyways?" Herm shook my hand, as he helped me grab the guard's equipment.

"I met someone really annoying."

He laughed in reply, "You need to tell me about it when we get a chance."

We made our way towards the coast, taking the alleyways and following the shadows, staying out of plain sight. My eyes would not stop their light, almost as if cursing me to chaos. It was difficult but Herm took the lead, and he became the eyes of our operation. It didn't take long before we reached the Legion, and they were all visibly annoyed.

"Ollius! You had us worried sick!" Sterg shouted.

"Keep your voice down! We're not in the clear yet." Herm interrupted.

Ochos, Nikolaus, and Aristos were already on the boat preparing for our trip alongside the Remnant the Legion had prepared for us.

I felt my stomach sink, deeper and deeper with every moment that flew by. I couldn't figure out why at first, but the realization slowly came to the surface.

"Where's Cilla?" I asked.

"She should be back soon. She said she had to take care of something and ran off." Sterg replied, turning away.

"How long ago was this?" I replied.

"Not long before you got here. Maybe an hour or two." Sterg answered.

"Which way did she go, Sterg?!" I shouted.

"Simmer down. It's Cilla. She can handle herself." He replied, signaling me to calm down with his arms.

"Which way?!" I gripped my fist, splitting the shield handle.

Sterg pointed behind me and continued, "She ran off that way, towards the market. Is everything okay?"

"I don't know." I shook my head, "I'm going after her. You guys stay here and be prepared to leave as soon as we get back." I ordered as I turned around and bolted towards the center of town.

"Ollius! Wait!" Herm shouted behind me.

I ran at a speed I didn't think was possible. It was definitely humane but unnatural. This wasn't the work of my crimson power—this was different. It wasn't an act of wrath or rage. I didn't feel any power rise up; it was just the Spartan blood within me pumping my every step.

I reached the market and hopped on top of a building to get a better look.

That's when I saw Cilla being surrounded by men. She was at a stall, looking for something. She had no idea of the threat that resided mere feet away. I couldn't tell, but it looked as if they wore no clothing. They were creatures built up of an abyss. I saw no light reflect off them. It was as if looking into a void. More menacing than the feeling I got from them, was the fact that they held no blade. They were surrounding a Spartan, a talented one at that, and carried no weapon. This put my mind into overdrive; I had to get there before they did.

I jumped off the home I stood upon and landed in a squatting position. I dashed towards the stall, praying I could get there before they could hurt her. I vaulted over stalls, and even entire homes.

I eventually found myself jumping over the stall and hiding inside the booth next to her.

"Cilla. You're surrounded." I whispered.

"Ollius? What're you doing here?" She replied, reaching for her dagger.

"No time to explain. Get ready to fight. There's six of them, they carry no blade, I think they were looking to rob you." I whispered, reaching for my sword.

I couldn't grab anything. It wasn't there. I must've dropped it when I ran here, I couldn't remember.

Cilla removed the shield off her back and handed me it.

"I trust you."

Those three words hit me like a spear. I felt my arms getting weak. I can't explain it.

I nodded my head, gripped the shield, and jumped over the table.

Three of them stood before me. It was then that I realized I wasn't hallucinating. These three that stood before me were nothing but a ravine of darkness. I couldn't see the end or the beginning. It was as if touching it would mean me falling into it.

"What do you guys want?" I asked, my shield at the ready.

There was no response. At least not verbally. I heard a voice in my head echo, "Die. Son of Sparta!" I could feel thousands of years of suffering within those words. Anguish, misery, despair. There aren't enough words to describe the echo that drove their sound. I relived those years in a mere second. These were tortured spirits.

One of them shot at me, their upper body extended, as the backside catapulted forward.

I raised my shield to meet it. I could see its friend getting ready to do the same before a dagger dove through it.

"Ollius, watch out!" Cilla shouted, as I ducked under, picking up the creature with my shield, I pounded it into the ground.

The daggered creature sent itself towards me. I looked behind, getting prepared to dodge before it exploded from within. A barrage of light shot through it, as the dagger returned itself to Cilla.

I looked behind me to see three of the creatures had already fallen to her.

She dashed forward, slashing the last creature, a bright light shot through it. It hollered but not in horror. It was a holler that told stories of imprisonment. For thousands of years, they were trapped. It was a holler of thanks. One of escape. I knew that holler very well.

I looked at her, shocked. I held the last creature below my shield. I kept pounding it with the edge of the metal that outlined her shield. It wouldn't disappear.

She walked over, throwing the dagger through the creature's head—releasing it.

I looked around for the third creature to find it was gone.

"Thank you." I said, removing the shield from its position.

"They're Death Omens, Ollius. If Death Omens are after us, we're in trouble." Cilla replied.

"Death Omens?" I asked, standing up.

"They're spirits that were banished from death. Meaning for hundreds of years, they suffered through complete isolation. They deteriorated over time. The worse their mental state is, the stronger they are." She replied, walking towards me.

"How'd you defeat them?" I asked.

She took her shield back before continuing, "This dagger was a gift from my father. It was the only thing he left me. It's called the *Upbringing*. It's one of the few weapons in existence that can kill a Death Omen."

I stood there; just thankful we were fine.

"Why'd you even come back here?" I asked.

"To get you this." She walked behind the table, grabbing something, and tossing it to me.

I caught the tunic that I was looking at earlier.

"You risked your life for it, I figured you'd want it." Cilla said, walking past me.

I stood there, gripping that tunic. It was the nicest thing anyone's ever done for me. It was a gift. I've never received one of those before.

"Thank you."

"We have to get going." She replied, coldly. However, I could sense a glimmer of happiness inside her voice. She walked with an excited emphasis in her step.

I walked besides her back to the Legion. I found my sword on the ground along the way. We told them about the Omens as we began to set sail.

"Death Omens, you say?" Sterg asked, stroking his long beard.

"Yeah. Cilla took out all six of them with her dagger." I answered, crossing my arms.

"We need to be wary. Death Omens are only the beginning." Sterg warned, looking out into the sea.

"Everyone keeps saying that. What's happening?" I asked, looking at Sterg with a frustrated look on my face.

"Hades' Wrath." He sighed. He turned towards me and leaned forward.

"We are in danger."

Chapter 8: Hades' Wrath

We began to set sail towards the island. The adventure at this point had been long, and the toll it took on our bodies was apparent.

It's about a day's trip that's left before we reach the island. That night, Sterg told me more about "Hades' Wrath" and what it entailed. Essentially, it was one of the three attestations of a disaster on a global scale. Hades' Wrath was the third sign—the God's intervention. If Hades' Wrath was directed at us, it meant we were on the wrong side of history.

We were in danger.

Before I was released, there had already been two signs that the Legion were made wary of. There was a large-scale famine, and the spontaneous destruction of the Jesters Wheel. The Jesters Wheel was a monument in Athens that fell apart on its own. Witnesses say they saw the Jester burn, as the wheel melted. Sterg told me that the Jester represented a time of peace. He was a sign from the Gods themselves. In times of peace, the Gods would place him in the most prominent city, as a sign of relief. When the Jester burns, it's a sign of apocalypse. Thomas took this as a sign that the revival of Sparta was close at hand, a sign that the Spartans' strength was to be feared by Greece. However—the Death Omens changed everything.

That night, I could not sleep. I was awake, thinking of a plan to stop Hades in his tracks. My mind raced for hours. The man in the field, the Death Omens—they were connected, I just couldn't figure out how. Worse still, I couldn't get that itch out of my mind. Something was bothering me; something didn't make sense and I didn't know what. I sat atop the boat, staring into the night sky for hours. Sterg had left Nikolaus to steer the boat as he got some sleep.

"Go get some rest, Ollius."

"I can't." I replied, a hint of worry in my voice, one that Nikolaus picked up on almost instantly.

"You're worried?" He asked.

"Who told you that?" I asked, turning my head towards him.

"You're shaking."

I looked down, and he was right. My hands shook. I couldn't keep them stable no matter how hard I tried.

There was a breeze in the air that spoke of warning. I stared at my palms as doubt and fear filled my mind. An idle movement in the silent night that surrounded us.

"Calm down." He reassured me, "You're worried for your comrades."

The splash of the water was the only thing that interrupted the silence.

"We forget we're human, Ollius, even you. Hades is a God—and one of the strongest at that. It's okay to be worried." He said, breaking the silence.

"I know that's scary to think about. A god—an actual one. We make temples for them; we sacrifice for them—some of us even pray to them. We never thought we'd be fighting them, but this is the hand we were dealt. It's either them, or us.

But don't underestimate us. Don't forget, we were bred for battle. This world turned its back on us, forgetting that we've got eyes there too."

There was another silence before I chimed in, "The day will come that the Legion will put their faith in me, I can feel it coming, the day of judgment. I don't know if I can handle it. If you asked me a week ago if I could, I'd promise you I can. But when I stood in that field, staring into those eyes. The man in the hood—I think that was Hades. I had never felt fear like that before. He investigated the deepest part of my soul and challenged it. He said he killed my father, and more importantly, I think I believe him. I don't want to risk the Legion for my ego. A battle with Hades could mean the end for all of us. The consequences would be dire."

"You're the strongest man I've ever met. I'd never say this in front of anybody, but I do trust you. Your strength is inconceivable. Your will is unlike anything I've ever experienced. When we fought, I got a taste of that, and I knew right then and there what you were capable of. That's why when you held my life within your palms, I smiled. When that day comes, we'll take down Hades together."

I stood up, walking towards him.

I grabbed his arm, shaking it.

I awoke the next day to a blazing sun. It was a hot day, and I had my brand-new tunic on. It was a maroon long-sleeve. It was made up of a soft material that made me feel so comfortable. We were on a course for the island, and it'd only been a couple of hours.

The boat we were on had two floors. There was the deck, and then a small compartment below where the rest of the Legion slept.

Cilla was bird watching behind me, as Sterg and Nikolaus bickered over who got to steer. That left Aristos and Hermaeus who were to the side of me playing Chess.

Then it hit me, where was Ochos?

"Hey Sterg!" I shouted.

"Yeah?"

"Where's Ochos?" I asked.

"Have you checked below? I actually haven't seen him all day now that I think about it."

I approached the compartment below and opened it.

Ochos was gone.

"Everybody! Ochos is nowhere to be found." I hollered as I turned back towards the group.

"Maybe he fell overboard?" Aristos chimed in.

"He's a trained soldier. He can swim. Not to mention, Nik was up all night, he would've seen something." I replied.

"Maybe he bailed then?" Herm said, looking up towards me.

"I almost killed him for being so dedicated to the mission Herm. I don't think he would just leave. I think he's in trouble." I replied, crossing my arms.

"Sterg. What do we do here?" I asked, looking towards him.

"I'm not quite sure. Did anybody hear anything last night?" Sterg asked the group.

"I didn't hear anything—but I did see something." Cilla said, walking towards our little huddle.

"What'd you see?" Sterg asked.

"I didn't want to say anything but, I awoke late at night to a man standing on the water." She answered.

"You said a man? Standing on water? You sure it wasn't a Death Omen?" Aristos asked, standing up.

"I'm sure. If it was an Omen, we'd have all been attacked. This was different." She answered, shaking her head, "It could've been Ochos."

"Now that I think about it. You said there were six omens back at the stall, but I only took out five."

"You mention this now, Cilla?!" I shouted in response.

"I thought you counted wrong!"

"Whoever it was, we need to get Ochos back." I said, a little angry.

"He'd want us to continue the mission." Sterg said.

"I don't care." I replied.

"We wouldn't even know where to start! All we know is we were visited by someone last night, and for some unknown reason, they took Ochos. That's not a lot to go on." Sterg explained.

"We can't give up on him." I interrupted.

"We won't—I promise you, we won't—but we're running out of time. We may not be the only ones searching for the artifact. The Gem was activated, that's why we could trace it. For all we know, they might be fleeing the island now! Do you understand what this means for Sparta?!" Sterg lectured.

"I understand—I promise if one more person acts like I don't, I'm going to lose it!" I hollered, "But

I know what it's like Sterg—to be left behind—to be taken!"

"We all lost something that night! It wasn't just you!"

"I lost eighteen years!" I interrupted.

"And I lost the love of my life!" Sterg shouted, tears growing.

"I lost everything. I lost my son, I lost my wife, I lost everything. They took everything!" He paused, before continuing, "I can't sleep. I can't eat. Sometimes I can't breathe. The Achaean League took everything from me. You think I don't want to tear apart their limbs—you think I don't want to hammer their heads in?!" Sterg continued, his fists shaking with anger, he looked down.

"But I don't. Because I know there's going to be a day where I can avenge them. There's going to be a day when I can tear apart that monster, Ladon—that name haunts me, but I still believe, because if I don't, then I risk everything the Legion has fought so long for." He looked up towards me, "And you need to do the same too. We will find Ochos, but that time is not

now. Now calls for action, we need to prioritize."
Sterg said, staring into my crimson eyes. His black,
cold, lifeless eyes told stories of the worst type of pain
you can survive. I felt my chest squeeze, as it pounded
for release. I felt disconnected from myself, I felt
disconnected from my body. A sheering, sharp pain
thrusted into my heart, leaving behind an empty shell.
It was cold, unbearably cold. Had he been living this
way? Fighting this freezing, bitter heart for years?
Here stood a broken man with nothing left to give. His
family was taken—slaughtered mere inches away—
and yet, he finds the power to wake up every day to
fight a losing battle—to clash with his inner demons as
he did for eighteen years.

Before I got to reply, Sterg spotted land behind
me.

"We're here." Sterg said, as he walked past me
to grab the oar, preparing to stop the boat.

I was speechless. As much as it hurt, I knew he
was right. We had to go on without Ochos, at least for
the time being.

We eventually did reach the island. It was
mostly forest. I could see the trees climb to an altitude

that rivaled Zeus. The idea that we were supposed to look for a single Gem in a forest of this size was appalling. The trees were a beautiful shade of green, the leaves bright, the trunks healthy. It was odd how colorful and inviting a forest could be. Especially one with no inhabitants.

We hopped off the boat, our weapons sheathed.

"Everyone. Stay close." Aristos announced from behind.

"Aristos, prepare a plan to find this Gem. Herm, go on ahead and see if you can find anything. Take Ollius with you for protection. Cilla, you stay with Nikolaus, Aristos and I. Nikolaus, I need you to prepare the boat, keep an eye out for any visitors." Sterg ordered, none of us transgressed. Hermaeus and I went on forward, weary of what this bright green forest was to bring.

We walked for a few minutes, neither of us speaking.

"I genuinely don't know how we're going to find this Gem. The forest is just too big for five people to search." Hermaeus said, trying to create conversation.

"I know. It's not going to be easy, but what choice do we have?" I replied.

"Well, I guess we could—" Hermaeus stopped abruptly, throwing his hand at my chest, stopping me in my tracks.

"Everything okay, Herm?" I asked before I looked forward, my jaw dropping.

"Herm. What is this?"

"Scary." He answered, ominously.

In front of us was a line. Ahead of the line was a dead forest. It was burnt to a crisp. The trees were darkened, the leaves were gone. Ash, and other debris were splattered everywhere.

That wasn't what was eerie though. It was the fact that just across this line, life itself stopped.

"You think this has something to do with the Gem?" I asked.

"Definitely."

We went back to the group, as fast as we could. We had to let them know before someone stumbled upon the dead acres of forest. We were afraid of what would happen if we crossed the line ourselves. Luckily, as we reached headquarters, everyone was there, apart from Ochos of course.

"There's a problem. There's a big problem, Sterg." Herm said, out of breath.

"Ollius." He huffed and puffed, "Please explain."

I chuckled. "Not far behind us, there's a line that seemingly cut off life from this portion of forest. The trees are ashy, and dead. The leaves are gone, it looked as if there was no life past that line. We think it's got something to do with the Gem."

Sterg said nothing as he tapped Aristos, signaling him to come with.

I looked at Cilla as she shrugged and followed. Hermaeus did the same, before I decided to follow too.

We got to the line after about fifteen minutes of walking.

"You weren't kidding. That's creepy." Sterg said, bending down close to the line.

"What could do this?" Herm asked.

"Not sure. It's nothing I've ever come up against." Sterg answered, puzzled.

"I have a bad thought." Aristos announced. We all turned towards him, ready for the bad news.

"What if that's not what's being affected by the Gem?" He said, crossing his arms in discomfort.

"What do you mean?" I asked, my ears perked.

"Well. There's a reason nobody visits this island. This island has always been destroyed. Life was taken away after the first Jester disappeared hundreds of years ago. This was where the Gods placed the first Jesters Wheel. It was outside of Kavala and could be seen by all its citizens. One day, before the first War of Nations, the Jester's life was struck down by a bolt of fury. It destroyed all life on the island. That's the curse. If you spend too much time on this island, you will die. For hundreds of years, nobody dared step foot here." Aristos explained.

"So, how do you explain all this? These leaves are the brightest I've ever seen." I asked.

"I'm getting there—and look, I know this is going to sound insane, but, what if the Gem is responsible for bringing life back to this island?"

"Aristos. You're talking about a curse from the Gods. They wield world-ending power." Herm chimed in.

"I know but look!" Aristos said, running towards the line, "There's a curve. We're inside a circle, Hermaeus."

Sterg took a step back, "This Gem can revive the dead. It can unbind a curse from the Gods." Sterg stood in disbelief.

We all stood there for a while. It could've been anywhere from a minute to an hour. This was unlike anything anyone's ever experienced. A single Gem that rivaled the power of the Gods themselves. This much power was too much for one man to wield.

"What're we getting ourselves into here, Sterg?" Herm spoke.

"We should get started on finding it." Cilla said, breaking us out of our daze.

"Yeah. Yeah—you're right." I said, still a little out of it, "Aristos, how do we find this?"

"Well. I guess four of us can stand in all four directions and start walking towards the center. That's where we should find the Gem."

So, we did just that. We all headed towards our corner. I took the North, Hermaeus took the South, Cilla took the West, and that left the East to Sterg. Aristos had some crazy tools to help us find the right angle for our corner. It didn't really matter where we stood, just as long as we were perfectly across from each other. As soon as we dispatched, Aristos had us all independently count to four hundred. He figured that was long enough for us to reach our corners.

After counting to four hundred, I began walking towards Hermaeus. I spent that time thinking about the Gem, and what kind of power it held. It was enough firepower to bring Sparta back, sure. However, that was also the problem. That power *had* to corrupt any that used it.

Eventually, I reached this log cabin. It was made of the same beautiful wood. Even after they've been chopped down, they carried their healthy color. It was an odd display of life.

I saw Cilla and Sterg each to their own respective sides of the cabin. I figured Hermaeus was just across from me.

Before I got a chance to talk with Sterg or Cilla, I heard a rumble from inside the cabin.

I ran to the other side as fast as I could, but the door was already open, and Herm was nowhere to be found.

I felt my stomach sink.

I bolted through the door to see Herm standing over a man.

The man was of average build. He had dark black hair, and a beautiful shade of green for eyes. Although, he was terrified of the monster that stood over him.

"Herm. What's going on?" I asked, reaching for my sheathe.

"This is the guy. He has the Gem, and he won't give it to me." Herm replied, a voice of envy and lust.

"We don't know that he does—"

"No. I do—and you can't have it." The man replied.

I walked over, ready to force it out of him.

"Back off! You're not taking the Gem from me." Herm threatened.

I was shocked, Herm never had the guts to speak to me like that before.

"This isn't you--"

"You don't know me!" He shouted, interrupting me.

"Give me the Gem, now!" Herm continued, grabbing the man by his collar.

"You can't have it! I won't give it to you! I'll never give it up!" The man replied, a narcissistic whine screeching from his vocal cords.

I walked over, pulling Herm off him.

"Let go of me Ollius! I have to get that Gem." Herm repeated, grinding his teeth.

"Enough. Go outside. I'll get it for you." I said, throwing him towards the door.

"You'll just take it for yourself—"

"Think before you speak. Walk away while you still can Herm." I warned.

Herm hesitated for a second. As if trying to find the courage to stand against me before he walked off.

I looked towards the man, who now sat a few feet away from me.

"I can kill you and then tear apart your cabin finding the Gem. Either give it to me now, or I'll break your neck."

"You don't scare me." The man said, reaching below his bed.

I ducked behind a dresser as he launched a wave of piercing wind towards me.

It missed, barely. I looked behind to see a chunk in the heavy wood gone. It tore apart actual logs.

I grabbed my shield, preparing for battle.

"Don't come inside!" I shouted from the newly carved hole in the wall.

I turned, bolting towards the man, knocking the Gem out of his hand with my shield.

I grabbed him by his neck, throwing him towards his bed, breaking it.

I picked up the Gem, immediately feeling a sense of divinity within my arms. It was intense if I were to describe it in a single word. It radiated energy that of a God. It felt holy, and divine. It felt as if this Gem had the answers to everything human. Not only power, love, and life, but even scarier it had the answers to wrath, hate, and death too. The power reminded me of a deceiving light, the same one that stole me from my father as a child. But I was blessed with strength, and I wouldn't let that be decided by a Gem.

"Please, I'm begging you. I can't live without it." The man's voice rang throughout the cabin.

"What do you mean?" I asked.

"It's forbidden fruit. I can't go back to normal life after witnessing the strength of a God." The man said, wiping his tears, "I never used it to destroy, because I knew once that energy surged through my veins—I wouldn't be able to stop. Every moment I spend without it is unbearable pain. I need it back. I need it back!" The man shouted, sprinting towards me.

I swung my fist forward, knocking him clean out.

The power it controlled was dangerous. Not just for other people, but for the beholder themselves. When you taste that forbidden fruit, it ruins everything you'll ever taste again. No matter what you hold, it will never compare to that power. Whether it be a blade, bow, or even a staff. You'll be left an empty shell of who you used to be. A desperate plea for the power you lost ringing through your head every waking moment.

I knew what had to be done, and it killed me knowing I'd be the one to do it.

"Please." I heard sobs from below, "If you won't give it back, kill me."

I'd taken plenty of lives before, but none had asked me to.

This was one of the most difficult things I'd ever done.

"What's your name?" I asked, clenching the Gem, facing away.

"Narcissus." He replied.

"What's your tale, Narcissus?" I asked, as I grabbed the handle of my blade.

"I don't have one. I was too busy to make a family. I was too busy to start a life. I lead a poor existence. One of greed, envy, and lust. I abandoned my friends, my family all to seek a power I could never truly comprehend."

My heart ached for him, "What were you too busy with?"

There was silence.

"Myself."

"Then, Narcissus. Think of yourself in your final moments."

The man began to weep, although silently. He wiped his tears, prepared for what's to come.

"If it means anything. I'm sorry it had to end this way." I said as I raised my blade.

Moments later, I walked outside the cabin. My sword sheathed; the Gem clenched safely within my fist.

It was raining. Clouds thundered above me as I took the first of many steps towards my friends. The air grew cold, the sky grew alone. Raindrops splashing on the green, lively leaves of the forest, splashing on the grass filled dirt below me. Puddles of mud and other disgusting insects rose all around the cabin. Inside, lied a man—with a story unknown to both me and him.

Unfortunately, he wasn't my friend to bury.

I eventually arrived to my crew. They all asked questions, none of which got replies.

Cilla stood behind them. Staring at me with eyes of pity. She knew what I must've had to do in there. They all passed us, heading back towards the boat.

I gave Cilla a fake smile, it was all I had for her.

"Don't." She spoke.

"Hmm?"

"If you're upset, that's fine. I don't care if you lie to me, just don't you dare lie to yourself. We all do our fair share of that. Aren't you tired of it?" She replied.

I had no words for her, I merely walked away—as awkward as it was.

It didn't take long for us to reach the boat. The crew was excited to bring back something for Thomas. Apparently, this was a big deal for the Legion. I could understand why myself having held the power of the Gem. I knew I had to talk to Herm, however. I wasn't sure if he was still envious of the power.

On our trip back, I cornered him downstairs.

"Herm. We need to talk."

"No, we don't. Don't worry, I know I was acting recklessly back there. The Gem had some sort of hold against me. It called me. I'm sure if I had touched it, it would've been worse." Herm said, taking a bite of a crisp pink pomegranate as he passed me by, putting his hand on my shoulder, "I'm just glad you stepped in when you did."

"Yeah, it's no problem." I replied, as he walked away.

I was confused. To Narcissus, the mere thought of losing the Gem drove him into a frenzy. To the point where the thought of never having it again was worse than having a sword pierce his skull. Then, here stood Herm, good as new. It was odd, and I just had to believe Narcissus carried a weak will.

I wish I had pried more. I wish I had found out what was going on inside Herm right then and there. But, as all things mortal, everything comes to an end. I've grown to find beauty in the end.

We arrived at land safely. I knew I had to search for Ochos, but I couldn't risk anyone else holding the Gem. Its compelling nature was far too powerful of a weapon. I had decided to let the Legion take me back to their fortress, deliver the Gem safely to Thomas, and head back myself to search for him. It was the only way.

The trip back was long. We circled around Kavala, ignoring the city, and instead took to crossing the river. We didn't want to risk another disaster. We walked for days, Herm became distant, although he was still himself. We joked, and talked for hours, but there was just something different about him after the incident with the Gem. Maybe it was how I saw him, or maybe how he saw me. I made my second mistake when I decided ignoring it would be the better choice.

We took the long way around the Forest of Mares too—deciding to not risk another incident there as well. The creatures inside that forest were deadly. They tore apart Daniil's psyche and would likely do the same to any of us given the opportunity.

Not long after we passed the Forest, the Legion's camp was in plain sight. It's been a week or two since I've last seen it. We were all exhausted, even me—although mine was mental.

I couldn't get the cries of Narcissus out of my head. I couldn't figure out why he had impacted me so much—I just knew he did.

We walked up to the gates of the Legion, as Herm shouted up for Ant.

The gate swung open, providing us an entrance to the Legions fortress. I missed it, to be frank. I missed the smell, the people, the atmosphere. I missed having a home. The crew dispersed, all heading towards their barracks, except Sterg and I. We had a meeting with Thomas we couldn't afford to miss.

I followed Sterg towards the town hall, still a bit confused on how to find anything within these walls.

The door opened yet again to a quiet room. Thomas nowhere to be seen.

"Thomas!" Sterg hollered throughout the building.

I heard footsteps above. A woman of mid-thirties climbed down the stairs.

"Myrta. Always a pleasure to see you." Sterg said, giving the stranger a hug.

"It's good to see you back in town, Sterg. Thomas is just upstairs working on some stuff." She replied, her voice carefree and happy.

"Stuff?" Sterg asked.

"He wouldn't tell me." She laughed, "Well. I've got to get going now, stay safe!" Myrta said as she passed us.

The door closed behind her, again enveloping us into the same silence from before.

"Who was that?" I asked.

"That's Thomas' wife Myrta. She's a really nice person. Hard to believe she'd marry a stubborn guy like Thomas, but love is complicated." Sterg answered, chuckling.

"That's funny. Come on up here." A voice ordered from above.

I followed Sterg up the stairs into Thomas' office.

"You're back?" Thomas asked, uplifted, and excited.

"Not all of us, sir." Sterg said, carrying his words with weight.

"We lost Ochos." I chimed in.

A wave of sadness took over Thomas' face before asking, "And the mission?"

"A success. Ollius here's got the stone." Sterg answered.

I pulled a white silk bag from my pockets and tossed it on Thomas' desk.

"No matter what you do. Do not touch that stone." I warned, walking away.

"Wait." Thomas stood up, "There's something you both need to know about."

"What is it? I've to get going—Ochos was taken—"

"It's about Ochos." He interrupted, picking up his head to stare into mine.

I crossed my arms, worried.

"He showed up at camp—a few days ago." Thomas continued.

"Good. So, I'll see him on the training grounds." I said, turning away yet again.

"I never said he showed up alive, Ollius." Thomas interrupted.

I stood still. Time stood still. The door to his office swung slowly. Sounds of the house settling tore through the walls. Everything became so apparent to me at that moment. It was as if I was seeing everything twice.

What did he just say?

"What?" I asked, facing the door.

"Ochos. He showed up a week ago in the middle of camp. He was strung up to a pole, his arms torn off."

There was a silence as me and Sterg shared a look.

"Thomas. A week ago, we were stuck on a boat off the coast of Kavala." Sterg said, chiming in.

"It was exactly a week ago." Thomas reassured.

144

"What could cover such a distance that far so quickly?" Sterg asked.

If it was capable of killing a talented warrior like Ochos so quick, and so ruthless. Why didn't it take the rest of us? We were all asleep. Some of us didn't even have our blades. Why was Ochos chosen? Why not me? I didn't have any words for Thomas. I didn't have anything left to say. I looked at Sterg, hoping he knew how I felt. He nodded back at me, signaling me to leave.

That's when I was reminded of the Hooded Man's words.

I'd suffer a thousand deaths—but none would be my own.

The rest of the day was a blur. I remember leaving the town hall and just walking. I think I walked for hours. I walked to the training grounds, to the school, to the infirmary. I just needed to walk. I needed something constant. I reflected back on the trip, to the island, the forest, even back to my cage. My life was my own, but at the cost of my comrades. Daniil was in pain. Ochos was gone. Hermaeus, my best friend, was nowhere to be found. He was distant, and cold. Ever since the incident with the Gem, I felt the separation between us grow. Maybe it was envy, maybe greed. I wasn't sure.

It was now late at night, and the sky was yet again filled to the brim with stars. I paused while crossing the bridge.

There was a specific constellation that stood out to me. It was a sword. Demetris had told me this one before, although I've never seen it before. It gave me a feeling of belonging. I stood there for a while staring at it. I couldn't explain it, but although I've never seen the constellation before, I have seen that blade. Better yet—I've held it.

I eventually did reach the barracks. Herm was up, waiting for me.

"Where've you been, Ollius?" He asked, throwing a ball up and down.

"Out." I answered, heading towards my room.

"Not so fast, Beast." Herm said, stopping me in my tracks,

"Tomorrow, early. We've got a meeting with Thomas."

"About what?" I asked, now looking down at Herm.

"Not sure. Might be about the Gem though."

I walked past Herm, excited to hit my bed. I had a long trip, and my body was craving some actual sleep.

I closed my eyes, thinking about everything. I thought about Daniil's condition, Ochos' death, Tri's blade, even Narcissus. I was ready to close my eyes and forget for a couple of hours. I thought back to the cage. In only a couple weeks, my life changed. For the most part, it was for the better. I had my freedom, and I had friends. I just felt responsible for everything now. I felt responsible for the lives, and the deaths of my comrades. Back in my cage, I was alone. I had Demetris to talk to, and no one to worry about.

I finally managed to drift away into a deep sleep.

In all my years, I've never dreamt but that all changed when I dreamt of a special someone that night. No, not Calista—I dreamt of the man in the robe. He visited me.

I was in a dark forest, alone. I heard laughter from all around, maybe it was my brain paying homage to what happened to Daniil. It was terrifying, and it only got worse when I saw the hooded man rise from behind the bushes.

That's when I woke up to banging on my door. I reached over to the dagger I had placed next to my bed as fast as I could.

"Ollius! Wake up!" A voice hollered from the other side.

"I'm up! I'm up!" I yelled as I pulled open the door.

"There's a problem. Grab your gear, get to the town hall now!" Herm screamed at me as he ran to the exit.

I reached over to the side of the door grabbing my blade and a white shirt. I put it on as I dashed away towards the door.

Just over the horizon I sensed it.

A peculiar power—but not one that reminded me of Hades' Wrath.

Death was marching.

Chapter 9: The Siege

I heard shouts and screams from civilians as I ran as fast as I could towards the Town Hall. I saw citizens of the Legion crying, shouting for their loved ones as the bells rang in the background. Kids, parents, elderly all running for the school, hoping to find shelter.

I pounded on the Town Hall, almost breaking the door down before it shot open to a determined Thomas staring back at me. He pulled me in, stretching my shirt in the process.

"What's going on? People are scared out there!" I shouted, seeking answers.

Inside stood Thomas, Sterg, Herm, and Aristos.

"Shut up! We've sent Nikolaus to protect them at the school, and we have Bryon and the other archers stationed all around the fortress. Matullus felt a presence over the mountains, something big—like a cavalry. We're getting ready to defend a siege." Thomas explained, turning around.

"Where is Matullus now?"

"He's in the infirmary. He mumbled something about evil incarnate and passed out with whitened eyes. We have our doctors looking at him now. We're blind to what's out there." Thomas explained.

"Herm—do you still have the robe?" I asked, turning towards him.

"Did you forget? We lost it after you got locked up Ollius." Herm replied, attitude rang through his voice.

I exhaled, angrily.

"What do we do here Thomas?"

"We fight. It's as simple as that. Sterg—gather some men. Ollius—grab your circle and take the Seventh with you. Divide them between the West and the East of the fortress. Aristos—we must come up with a plan now." He emphasized, "This is life or death—more importantly if we lose today, it'll mean the end of the Spartan race." Thomas ordered as we all broke.

I dove through the door as I ran back towards the barracks, swinging my arms as fast as I could as I sprinted past the courtyard.

The streets were less cluttered now, the main population seemingly evacuated into the school.

I ran into Cilla along the way. I instructed her to grab the Seventh Circle and to split them up in between the West and the East of the fortress.

I looked at my blade as she bolted away. It was dull, the edge rusted and the handle almost crushed.

It was about time I got to let my Crimson Rage soar yet again. I felt my heart pulse with excitement as I anticipated the upcoming battle.

A roar rang through the mountains from the West. They were closing in.

That's when it hit me. The roar of the beast rattled something inside my mind—what was bugging me this entire time, from the day I stepped outside of Mizeria, to the minute I fell asleep last night, became clear. That aching feeling behind my inner consciousness finally subsided. I knew what I had to do—and I knew I had what it took.

As I stared into the twilight of the night sky, I felt a tap on my shoulder.

Rain poured in the hundreds of gallons as I turned around, seeing Nikolina look back at me.

"Thomas told me you'd need me. What's the plan?" She asked, in a rush.

"Head over the Town Hall—before you do, I need you to relay a message to Cilla for me."

"But—"

"This is important, Lina. Please." I begged—interrupting her.

"Have them all, the entire Seventh at the East side of the fortress." Rain began splashing down upon us.

"Ollius. Are you sure?" Nikolina pressed.

"Go."

"But Ollius—"

"I said go!" My voice exploded through the fortress. My eyes, enveloped in the same red prowess from before. Strength, like that of an ox ran through me. I felt heat engulf my fists, and a beautiful relief crawl up my spine. I no longer had to hold back.

I ran towards the West, as Nikolina ran towards the East.

It's hard to explain what I had prepared for the cavalry. I was one man, how was I to defeat an army? Even with my seemingly unlimited strength—it was impossible. I was risking everyone's lives on a whim. Leaving an entire side undefended. However, playing it safe is the riskiest choice you can make, and it took a while for me to fully comprehend that.

I arrived at the West and began scaling the wall.

Once I arrived on top, I saw the army.

Gigantic waves of enemies stretched as far as the eye could see. They were armed with red swords, and other red weaponry. Their faces, disgusting. Their eyes, every single one, full of greed and envy. Their skin was green, and their ears rounded up top like a bear.

What stood before me was against anything humane. Demetris told me about these creatures—Goblins—as he described them. There were gigantic ones in the front, the ones I assumed were for knocking down the walls. Some rode horses, some rode warthogs. Some held bows, far in the back, and on the side of the cavalry.

The center of them all stood one man.

One man, in a black robe.

I looked upon them, as they closed in. Every step they took only warned me of the chaos they wished to bring. Every swing of their tiny short arms only threatened my sanctuary. Every smirk they shared only promised to take my home.

I shouted. I roared. I screamed. Whatever it took to remind the resonating doubt in my heart that *I* would not lose. Whatever it took to remind the dull blade in my arms that failure was not an option for *me*. I *am* the impossible—I *am* the inevitable. I rose from the dark confines of my cell to remark upon this world my power—to create a new fear for every child and man. I am Ollius, and my voice *will* be heard so that my name may *never* be forgotten again.

I was angry, I was furious with them. I found a home, friends, maybe even family—and they wanted to take it. Every step they took closer to my home only further pushed me towards the edge.

They will suffer.

There was no room for error. This was the final stand. Between the vanguard and the walls stood me. I wouldn't let them pass.

In my anger, red smoke arose from around me. It was a large mass of red fog. I felt anger rise from beneath it—heating up the air itself. Suddenly, a fire erupted. An army emerged, standing up from a knee. The same strong physique, the same red, crimson eyes. The same egotistical chip on their shoulder. It was an army of me. This was how I took down Mizeria—I remembered it all so clearly now. Those memories of my battle were not collected by me alone. That itch at the back of my head finally dissipating.

I smirked, dropping down to the other side of the wall, ready to lead my men to the fight of their lives.

I looked around to the hundreds of soldiers built from me—the pinnacle of beauty and perfection—looked back. I raised my blade to the air,

"Tonight. We dine in their blood!" I shouted, as the men shouted back in unison.

I led my men in a war cry, dashing towards the Goblin army.

I don't remember much from the battle. I swung my blade thousands of times. This singular, steel blade had led me through another massacre. I slashed, digging deeper inside every one of these selfish, greedy creatures. They begged, even pleaded for me to stop—but I kept swinging. I never stopped shouting. My anger never subsided. They stood with the man in the robe—that's all I needed.

"Die! Die! Die! You'll all die!" I screamed as I plunged my sword through the skull of a giant one. I'm not sure which soldiers' memories I was remembering. All of us—every soldier of mine shed their fair amount of blood. Till dawn, I kept slashing. The men of the Legion tried to help to no avail. The Goblins were physically stronger and faster than any mere human. Every single one of their attempts proved useless. They took to aiding their archers and sorcerers to help me push back the army.

No amount of killing was helping. No matter how much I chopped through, the herd kept growing. The man in black was nowhere to be seen—this worried me.

I heard the roar from the creature yet again riding through the mountains. Whatever was making that sound was making its way here, and fast. I had to end this quick,

We all jumped back, raising our blades to the air.

"Build a barricade, drive them back!"

I dove back in, I swung, killing one. I hopped atop another, kicking his face into the ground below as I countered another's attack breaking his nose. Whatever I'd come up with, I had to come up with it soon. Time was running out, and the Goblins kept coming.

That's when it hit me—the Gem was the only thing with enough power to take their army out.

I arrived at the Fortress where Sterg stood. He and Aristos stood atop the wall, crossing their arms, surveying the situation.

"They keep coming, Sterg. I don't know what to do." I said, out of breath.

"Are you doing okay?"

"I don't know. I've never been tired before." I replied, downing some water.

"I don't know what to do. There's just too many of them." Sterg said, breaking my spirits.

"The Gem! I think it might be the key to ending this. Where is it?" I asked, grabbing my knees in discomfort.

"Thomas has it. Last I saw, he was walking Hermaeus to the school."

"That's not good. Where are they now?—" I was interrupted by thunder clapping behind me.

I felt all the energy I exerted summon back to me in an instant.

I looked around to see a storm brew atop the cavalry, destroying its forces. From the giants to the archers—the army was disintegrated in a single attack.

I turned around, looking to Sterg for answers.

"That's not any Spartan magic I've ever seen." He spoke, my heart collapsing.

"I was afraid you'd say that." I said as I looked around for the culprit, although I had an idea of who it might be.

Below the wall stood Hermaeus, clenching the Gem within his palms. The power of life and death, fire, and water, even good and evil stood mere feet below me. He had touched the Gem—moreover—he had used it in battle. He had cursed himself.

"Herm! What did you do?!" I shouted.

Herm looked up, confused.

"I took out the cavalry, Ollius."

"Not like this. Not at the cost of your soul." I said as I leapt down to meet him.

"What are you talking about?" Herm argued.

"Hand over the Gem." I said, extending my hand towards him.

"That's not happening." Herm said, clenching the Gem harder than before, pulling it to his chest.

"You risked all our lives here—more importantly you tainted yours. Hand over the Gem, before I am forced to take it!" I shouted.

"This is my power Ollius!" He emphasized, "I'm not giving it up."

I sent a fist towards his nose, breaking it— knocking him off his feet.

I got atop him, wrestling for the Gem.

"Ollius, get off of him!" Thomas ordered from behind me.

"Thomas. This power is dangerous!" I shouted back.

"Dangerous or not, we need it."

"The cavalry's gone! We need to save him from this—"

"That's not what I was talking about. Look." Thomas interrupted, pointing to the west, over the mountains.

The roar returned—bouncing off the vast eminence over the horizon. I saw a creature rise over them. Crimson wings soared, contrasting the light gray sky. Miles away, it only made the size of the Dragon more impressive. Its red eyes shot daggers towards the Fortress, with sharp white teeth as bright as moonlight. The creature curled its wings into its body, enveloping it into flames.

I let go of Herm, standing up slowly. I couldn't figure out how to summon my army again once

Herm's blast turned them to ashes. I felt too exhausted to conjure up more.

I looked back to Sterg. He stood; his jaw wide open. I know he'd defeated a Dragon before, but now seeing one as terrifying as this—it felt impossible. It was humongous and threatening. Its sheer size alone was something to behold. The flame it controlled was impeccable. Echoes of a burning blaze surrounded it. Something about the creature declared a genius that we all feared.

If I could not take down this Dragon, it would mean the end for everything. From the people to the walls—this place accepted me. Ever since I first arrived here, I felt a sense of welcoming. They saw me as one of their own and not a tool to be used for battle. I did not want to see this place fall. I would die before I saw this place fall.

I was now standing, clenching my blade. Dull, weak, and ineffective at this point. Towards the end of the battle, I was using it as a mere blunt object. It's gotten me far enough; it was time to put it to rest. I approached a nearby boulder, driving my blade into it, eternalizing today's battle.

I looked around to see my teammates. I saw Stergious, our commander. I saw Thomas, our leader. I saw Cilla, a warrior of fine strength. I saw Hermaeus, now tainted with the Gem. Nikolaus, even Bryon too. If it meant our lives, this Dragon will be slayed by the end of night.

I took my first steps towards it before I was stopped in my tracks.

"Wait!" An unfamiliar voice rang.

I looked back to see it was the kid that had let me borrow his blade the first time.

"I'd be honored if you'd take my blade again." The kid said, handing me the hilt.

"That way—you'll be forced to win."

I smiled, "What's your name kid?"

"Isaiah of the Fort."

"Take care of things back at the school for me, Isaiah." I patted him on his back, as he nodded in confirmation.

I turned towards the Dragon that was now ready to launch towards us.

"Bryon. Station your archers in the corners of the Fortress and on the mountain sides that surround us." I ordered.

"But he's so far—shouldn't we bring the attack to him?"

"Yeah, I'm going to agree with Bryon, Ollius. It's too dangerous to fight him here." Sterg agreed.

"Did you forget this was a siege? We're defending the attack. If we go on the offensive—we'll be at a disadvantage. He's a lot more mobile than us. We can't risk not being here to defend our city. We need spears, and catapults. Bring them out now! Station them all around the fortress—not inside it." I lectured, turning away back inside the Fortress.

I was ready for what the Dragon would bring. Death, destruction, and merciless killing, but was that different from any other day in this cursed world? Baylor was built to be destroyed. I was prepared to do anything, and everything it'd take. The question remained; would it be enough? Was I acting carelessly? Was I even fit to lead?

It didn't matter. Whether or not I was at the helm, men would die today.

The men of the Legion had prepared everything for the defense. They gathered around the West entrance at my discretion.

"Men and women of the Legion. For all the preparations, we've still forgotten one thing. The fact that we're not doing this for Sparta's revival." I was met with some confusion in the audience before I continued, "We're doing this for Sparta's *survival*. Sparta's here. It's been here. Within every one of us lies the Will of Sparta—it never died! There is an ember inside all of us, a burning flame that reminds us of home—that reminds us that tomorrow is not promised—it's guaranteed! We are Spartans. We were bred from strength—it's as simple as that. Today marks the day we stop letting Greece control us! We will no longer hide; we will no longer run! You have my strength, and I have yours! If we die today, it will not be here! We'll Ryse against any that stand among us!"

The soldiers roared in return. Yelling and screaming "Ryse!" all among the crowd.

I let out a chuckle at their asynchronization chants, "After we win today, we'll work on our coordination."

The Dragon hollered in the distance, emanating a voice of contempt and hatred. It was here to destroy; it had no other drive. Chaos, and death was the only thing that inspired it to soar.

I grabbed a spear, running towards the entrance as the crowd broke, heading towards their stations.

It was finally time. It was do or die—there was no other option. If we could not defeat this Dragon, it meant the end for all of us—but that mere thought was not enough to kill us.

Chapter 10: Final Stand

Flames erupted all around me, from the walls to the homes of the Legion. There was devastation around every corner. Death and misery and everything in between. I heard screams and shouts for help, as I sat helpless clenching the blade in one hand, and the Gem in the other. I shed a tear. I felt the taste of copper within my mouth as I held the lifeless body of a comrade. This meant war. I couldn't let Hades get away with this.

It all started when we broke to our stations. I remember grabbing the spear and dashing towards the beast. Time slowed down as I felt my veins pulse. The air around me screamed as I felt my body force itself past exertion. I charged my spear back, aiming it towards the Dragon.

I saw Hermaeus stand atop the wall, presenting the Gem towards the beast, getting ready to strike it with all his might.

However—it didn't work. None of it worked. Not my spear, not the arrows, not the catapults. The Gem was worn out. After a strike like before—maybe it needed time—we weren't sure. It all happened so fast. I threw the spear as it merely bounced off the beast. It dove into the barricades, launching Herm across the camp, his blade flying towards another part of the wall. I saw Sterg drop down towards the creature with his Warhammer. He blunted it atop its head, amounting to nothing. It sent him flying with a flap of its wings. The creature launched its flame all around us—burning everything down. I saw Nikolina trip over a fallen soldier. I saw Nikolaus run to help her as he caught wind of the flame. I grabbed my blade running towards it yet again. It looked back, its eyes shining. My crimson eyes locked with theirs. I swung my blade through its wings, shattering the steel into two.

Our eyes met, mere inches away. A battle of crimson—a battle of hate and wits.

I was thrown back by the creature as it flew up, producing more flame in its departure.

I couldn't let it hit—but I didn't know what to do. I was too weak to conjure up an army to shield us from the blast, and it was too high up to stop it myself.

I had no time to waste. I shot up, running towards the walls—I had an idea I just needed the right angle.

The Dragon soared through the sky, getting ready to dive yet again. I grabbed the broken blade by its hilt, aiming it towards the crystal in between its eyes. It was the only thing I could think of doing. I saw a target, and I knew I needed to hit it.

As the Dragon dove down, fire enveloping its tongue, I threw the hilt as hard as I could, my Crimson Rage taking control yet again.

I shattered the crystal—but not before it laid another flaming attack towards the Legion. I was too late. Pieces of the crystal scattered everywhere throughout the camp, including right next to me.

The Dragon fell back, retreating into the sky. It stared daggers at me. It knew what I did, and how much of a danger I was.

I heard Thomas scream towards me, "Ollius! It's going to dive again; you have to kill it!" He was trapped under some debris, just below the wall I stood upon.

I looked up, seeing the Dragon diving at high speeds yet again, but not towards me, it was diving towards Thomas. It had no flame this time, but the sheer size alone was enough to tear him to pieces. I had nothing to attack it with—how was I to kill a beast of this size with no weapon? That's when it came to me—Herm's blade was below me. I had one shot at this, I couldn't afford to miss.

I waited until the Dragon was close before jumping off the wall to meet its blood red eyes. While falling, I pulled Hermaeus' blade from the wall, as if what I was about to do was destiny. I swung the blade with all my might, its steel turning a bright red as I struck its eye, knocking it far away from the walls to the middle of camp. I held on with all my strength as the blade dug deeper inside its skull.

Nikolaus ran towards me, hoping to aid me in my battle.

The Dragon stood up, throwing me off its head.

I fell next to Nikolaus, as he helped me up.

I looked to him as he nodded. I nodded back. We were now standing face to face with the monster that destroyed what the Legion had built.

I was angry, fuming even. I felt the crimson aura return, enveloping my body.

I gripped Herm's blade in my right arm, as Nikolaus got into his stance.

I ran towards the beast, dodging its teeth as it reached to clench me within its jaws. I landed atop its head running alongside its back, stopping atop its right wing. I raised my blade swinging it with all my might, a bright red tint taking hold of its steel, preventing it from taking flight ever again.

It threw itself back in a wail of torment, hoping to crush me as I jumped to the other side.

If I could do that again—I'd leave it defenseless.

I landed on all fours, standing up and turning around to see its claws closing in. Whoever—and whatever I may be—I could not defend an attack like that. A singular claw alone was the size of me and powered by the Wrath of Hades.

My mind raced. Maybe I could try to block? Maybe cut off its claws? I had to try something!

Before I could react, through the chaos I saw only a hand pull me out of the way throwing me backwards. As if in slow motion I had fell back to see a streak of blood shoot towards me. I was dizzy, lightheaded even, having took a hit to the back of my head.

Gathering myself, I sat up to see Nikolaus mere feet away.

He was cleaved, blood the spotlight of his arms. He stood on his two feet walking towards me fighting against the sips of pain, even after an attack like that. He bled from all around his body. I wasn't sure how he was even standing. What inconceivable power ran through this man? He fell towards me, handing me the Gem in his final acts of strength. He looked at me, reaching up towards my eyes and settling for my collar, uttering his final five words,

"It's okay to be worried." He smiled for the last time. A simper I'd not soon forget.

Flames erupted all around me, from the walls to the homes of the Legion. There was devastation around every corner. Death and misery and everything in between. I heard screams and shouts for help, as I stood helpless clenching the blade in one hand, and the Gem in the other. I shed a tear. I felt the taste of copper within my mouth as I held the lifeless body of a comrade. This meant war. I couldn't let Hades get away with this.

In my peripheral vision, I could swear I saw a red rose spring up from the ground. Holding my deceased friend, I could only feel empty. Moreover, I felt guilty—as I looked into his cold dead eyes, the same thought uttered through my head repeatedly,

I had lost my friend. Nikolaus had given his life for me. I had lost my friend. I had lost my friend. I had lost my friend. Nikolaus had given his life for me—

Everything came to a halt. Time stopped; the beast paused; the men and women fighting alongside me ceased their battle as they all felt it. Who we were, as warriors, didn't matter—which side we stood on didn't matter. All that mattered now was this burning fury inside my heart—inside all our hearts. We lost a friend. We lost a brother. Moreover, our walls were destroyed. Our hopes vanquished; our truths, forgotten. To me, in that moment all I felt was a blinding rage. I was no longer the Beast of Baylor. I was simply my yearning for blood. My hands shook, my head ached, my fists plead. Whether or not I lived to see the end of this battle no longer plagued me. I could only see the Dragon now. Everything else, a blur. My thoughts, a chaotic violence. My rage, beseeching.

I had made friends. Friends I'd be willing to die for, and yet I failed to time and time again. I clenched my blade in unfiltered fury. Rage ran through my veins, replacing the adrenaline. My eyes aflame, my blade of fire, my heart of pure blaze, I let go of Nikolaus, his limp body landing next to the rose. His eyes staring into its crisp red petals, welcoming him to the afterlife. I looked towards the beast, as it fell back in pure fear. A killer instinct soared through the air. It tried to fly to no avail. It tried to run, but I was far faster. In an instant, I slashed away its heel. In another, I had jumped on its back drilling a hole through its chest using Herm's blade. It dropped forward, wailing a sound of pain and distress, wheezing, begging for another chance at life. It was trying to call others—but there was no one left. Not on my side, and not on its'. It laid, crying for help. I swung down my blade, blinding it. I had let myself trust others, and this is what it got me, feelings, and pain and now grief. I let them all down. The entire Legion was in flames, my friend died within my arms—this creature could not live—Hades could not live. If it killed me, I would be the one to send him to his grave. I couldn't forgive him. I did not care for his reason, I did not care for his status, or the consequences. I could only think of tearing him limb from limb. I wanted him to feel the same pain Nikolaus felt in his final moments. The beast finally took its last breath as I hopped off, walking towards my comrades.

Nor reason or rhyme could explain the massacre that bestowed itself upon me.

The Dragon is a creature of the Underworld. Matter of fact, the Dragon is symbolic of the Underworld. Only Hades can control them, beasts of a Gods will, and a battalion of strength—there was only one being that could be responsible for this attack. Said to be the architect of Death, and the bringer of the apocalypse—The God of the Underworld, Hades.

This was no victory. There is no honor in death.

I walked towards Thomas, picking up the debris, freeing him from his capture. Nikolina was inconsolable after the loss of her twin brother. Hermaeus was unconscious from the fall, and Sterg was surprisingly fine. He was one of the few that got away with no wounds. Of the 200 men that bore arms against the Dragon, only 70 got away with their lives. The children, women, and other citizens too weak to battle were all fine within the schools' walls. Sparta had taken a big hit today. We were all distraught and exhausted. Cilla had broken a foot off the initial dive of the Dragon. It would take us some time to get past this. Luckily, the Legions magic protects us from the outside world through illusion. It disguised the fortress from the outside world, blending it into the environment to anyone without Spartan blood.

I fell to my knees. Not of fatigue, not of damage. I couldn't explain it. I just needed a moment to compose myself. Within the past month, my whole world changed. I grew to love; I grew to hate. Life within those damp walls of the Pit were lonely, sure, but at least I didn't have anyone to let down. I was damaged. My head hurt, my eyes a waterfall of tears. I let out a roar, one of beasts with nothing left to lose. I hammered my arms into the ground, cracking it. I turned around to my back, my eyes filled with tears. I laid there for hours, just waiting.

The clouds parted, revealing a night sky. The Legion had begun to pick everything back up. Those who needed treatment got it, and those who were too late for treatment, were taken outside the walls.

I laid there though. Staring at the stars, hoping to make reason with what had happened today. I wanted an explanation. What was the point of having these heroes eternalized into the stars if they weren't around to protect us anymore?

What was the point of having immeasurable strength if it failed you when you needed it most? I had so many questions run through my mind. What if I had just parried the attack with my blade, instead of Nikolaus blocking it? What if I dug my blade into its heart instead of its eye? What if the Gem had worked? So many questions, so little answers. I was born to a cage, just to escape it and be trapped within freedom.

The moon was now high in the sky, as it approached midnight.

I heard footsteps walking towards me. Was it Calista? Was it Hermaeus? Maybe Sterg? I almost didn't care.

A blanket dropped next to me. I looked to the side to see that it was neither of them.

There stood Cilla. Her green eyes offering salvation.

She said nothing, she just laid next to me, staring into the night sky.

"You don't have to stay here." I spoke, my first words in hours.

"I know. I want to." She replied.

I broke a smile before shedding another tear.

"Everyone's thankful for what you did, you know. They're calling you the Son of Sparta now."

I remained silent.

"You did all you could."

"No. There was more I could've done."

"You're not a monster." Those words weighed on me, "If there was more that could've been done, you would've done it. We were faced with an impossible enemy; we did all we could, and we need to live with that."

She was right, and it hurt realizing it. Her words only dug a deeper trench inside my heart. I would never see Nikolaus or have the opportunity to clash fists with him again.

"I just keep thinking, 'why wasn't it me instead?'" I replied.

"I've been asking myself the same question. Not just tonight, but my whole life. These are the cards that we were dealt. You can either play your hand or wait to lose." She turned towards me, flashing her eyes.

"What do you choose?" I asked, still looking at the ground below, as an ant crawled towards me.

"Neither. I choose to fight. I say damn the cards if they're not in my favor. Even when the monsters are preying on us every night. Even when the pressure is heavier than my steel blade. I don't have any other choice.

I found that it's better to lose a moment, than to die in one."

Her words told me everything I needed to know. She was right. I was tired of losing, and I would no longer wait around for the next enemy to attack. I had to bring the fight to them, and I had to take them all out.

"I know what you're thinking and you're not doing it alone." She replied.

"I'm not losing anyone else."

"And what about me?" She asked.

"You'll be fine here."

I felt a teardrop wet my arm. I raised my hand to my eyes to see they were wet yet again.

"I'm not putting anyone else in danger, ever again." I replied, finally raising my face to meet hers.

Chapter 11: Ruins

A month passed by as we rebuilt the Legion. We had a Town Hall meeting to discuss everything that happened. From the Gem to the man in the black robe, to the goblins attack, even to the dragon's flame. It was decided that Hades would have to fall if we had any hope of reviving Sparta. The Circles were reassigned to make up for the loss in men. We went from an elite seven to a final four. I was assigned to the Fourth alongside Nikolina, Hermaeus, and Cilla. Sterg was promoted to Commander of the Army, essentially in charge of the rest of the soldiers that were not involved in a Circle. Alongside having the Circles, the Legion still had an army. The Circles handled missions and other conquests. The army handled the protection of the walls, and if time ever came to be, a siege of our own. Thomas had taken some serious damage to his right leg and was awaiting recovery. The doctors are saying he may never walk again. The citizens were unharmed, luckily. However, I grew angrier by the day. The day came when Thomas finally gave us the order to prepare for the assassination of Hades.

Daniil was out of recovery. He had recovered from the Mares hold on his psyche. Matullus, who I finally got to meet, had created a remedy to save him. Essentially it healed his mind, but it didn't rearrange the chemicals, or anything else, it just healed the damage. As if healing a broken arm, without setting it right. He didn't lose any consciousness, or any sanity, luckily. Instead, the exact opposite happened. He grew an obscure ability. It was hard to explain at first. We thought they were premonitions, but it turned out to be far better. It's not as if he could see the future, his mind just worked faster. It could see actions and register them far quicker, to a supernatural speed. He was not appointed to a Circle, instead Thomas thought it was best he honed his ability before riding out into battle.

Thomas was adamant we keep ourselves safe. The Legion took a big hit during the Dragons attack, and we couldn't afford to lose any more soldiers, especially the Legions' best ones. He was against it at first, but after I threatened to leave to defeat Hades by myself, he came around to the idea. After all, Hades attacked us once before, it was only a matter of time he'd lay another siege towards us.

A fire inside me was aflame, an ember of pain and anguish was lit. I kept repeating that day in my head, the cries of the injured, the wail of the deceased, the bitter taste of Nikolaus' blood in my mouth would never escape my consciousness. I was haunted by his sacrifice, and I couldn't help but believe it should've been me instead.

I owed it to him, and to the fallen. If nothing else, I will take down Hades. I vowed to make him suffer for what he did to my people. I will tear down his walls as he teared down ours. I will massacre his army as he shed ours. I will drive my blade through his chest, piercing his heart, as I did his beast. To bear arms against me and my loved ones was a crime I could never forgive.

Hades will suffer.

Thomas alerted us that the only way to get to the Underworld that he's aware of is to talk to the Sage that resides atop Mount Olympus.

Mount Olympus resided next to the remains of what Sparta was. In its glory days, Sparta was hailed as the defenders of Olympus, a mountain blessed by Gods, and said to be their home. That meant, to move forward, we had to go backwards—back to where it all began. We had to venture to Sparta and take back what's ours.

We set out on yet another cloudy, rainy day. The four that belonged to the Fourth Circle met at the exit of the Legions fortress. Past the gates, the Fourth were to be met with divine beasts and an adventure that would be remembered by all of the Legions warriors.

We left with our bags packed, and our eyes set on the head of Hades. Since the day of the siege, I could not get the thought out of my head; to destroy Hades was what I had breathed for. I was angry, to keep it simple. I craved destruction, I craved violence. I would wake up in the middle of night shaking. I needed to avenge Nikolaus. I needed to avenge Ochos. I needed to avenge anyone that had lost their lives battling that Dragon. Although extinguished, the flames burned inside my head. A constant reminder of what I had failed to do.

We made our way to Mount Olympus. We spent days hiking and climbing mountains trying to make it back to Sparta. After it's defeat, Greece had taken down any direct roads or paths to the ruins. *One day, I'd rebuild these with my own arms*, I thought to myself.

It took a week before we reached Sparta. During the week, I spent a lot of time planning out different strategies and other schemes to defeat Hades. From battle formations to proper sword technique, I dove through it all. To fight a beast like Hades, we had to be ready.

"Just over this mountain." I said, reaching for the loose rock just up ahead.

"How do you know?" Herm asked.

"I don't." I said pulling myself up.

Just over the mountain I saw a destroyed city. Homes, or what's left of them. I saw destroyed statues, and debris shot all around Sparta. I saw what I assumed to be the Town Hall burnt to a crisp. The gates destroyed as if by a rabid dog. I climbed down the mountain in haste, almost falling off.

Arriving to the gate, I saw the barracks of Sparta in pieces. I saw swords, bows, shields, all types of weaponry scattered around, some dug into the dirt below. I saw bodies of the fallen, as if they had only died today. Their skin was healthy, their blood fresh.

I was puzzled, and honestly a little uncomfortable. Sparta fell over eighteen years ago, how could the bodies be so healthy? They were gone, I knew by their cold, dead eyes—but the bodies were fresh. I walked past the fallen soldiers and their bronze chest plates. I walked amongst the fallen, and the debris and ruins of Sparta. I walked past homes, shops, schools even. The whole time, I thought to myself, *which of these homes were mine? Which one of these bodies were my fathers, or mothers? Maybe I had some brothers, and sisters?* That thought angered me. It fueled my rage even more than before.

I came across a very sad sight. A man held his son, both pinned to a wall by a single arrow. The man was trying to protect his dearest—instead they both fell. I shed a single tear, wiping it away before Herm and the rest caught up to me.

"This is terrifying." Herm spoke, his voice a mixture of horrified and depressed.

"I know." I replied, looking away.

"Do you know which ones your home, Herm?" I continued.

"I'm not sure. I was too young." He replied, his voice on the verge of breaking.

There was a silence as we all stood, staring into a pit of death. The Achaean League didn't even have the courtesy to burn their victims. They had let them sit, hoping they'd deteriorate. They had killed my brethren in hopes of shielding themselves from monsters. It's funny how that worked—because in doing so, they themselves became the monsters.

War was sad. No matter what, there's always casualties on both sides. Groups of men risked their lives trying to defend the word of one. Patriotism, strength, maybe even honor—it doesn't matter what you call it, it's still foolish at the end of the day. War was not the answer, and although I knew that to be true, my anger still sought after the blood of Hades. War was evil, but it was all I knew. Should I let this vendetta go? Or should I keep my word and tear Hades from limb to limb? Truth be told, I didn't have an answer for myself. I don't know if I even wanted one.

We walked through Sparta, towards the entrance of a palace. It was gigantic, one of the only buildings still standing. It looked to be some sort of mansion.

Inside, we found the deceased body of a King. We knew that, by the crown that he wore.

Ci could not control herself. Her tears submerged my tunic. I held her close, hoping to ease her pain, but I knew no matter what I did, it wouldn't matter. Her father sat mere feet away, a blade stuck to his chest as he sat upon his throne. His mouth was open, dripping blood even after eighteen years. His hair white as if changed with age. I held her head, embracing her as she cried for what felt like hours. Herm and Nikolina were gone, looking for their own families maybe. I never knew my parents, so I wouldn't know what to look for. Red eyes, and an abnormal amount of strength were not two traits that were common, even amongst Spartans.

Cilla eventually stopped, now sitting staring into her father's lifeless eyes.

No matter how I looked at it. I couldn't find a way where I could justify the actions of Greece, and the entirety of Baylor. They destroyed their enemies, true. However, they did it in such an inhumane way it was impossible to forgive them. To do this to another living being is horrific to think about.

That's when it hit me. This must be what the investigators felt when they arrived upon Mizeria, and what I left of it. I sat there, alongside Cilla regretting my actions. *I was a monster.*

Mizeria imprisoned me. They destroyed my chances of ever living a normal life, but how I reacted was far worse. I murdered hundreds of men that day. Anyone that stood in my way had to face the wrath of a long-forgotten battle. From the get-go, Nikolaus was right. I was a monster. I didn't deserve the happy ending, and I owed it to the people of Mizeria to suffer as they did. This cycle of violence would never stop. If I stopped now, that meant the lives I'd taken along the way meant nothing. If I didn't accomplish my goal of bringing back Sparta and killing Hades, then the fallen had died for no reason. I was the vessel of my own arrogance. I was the vessel of hate. I became a monster somewhere along the way and justified my actions because I too suffered.

I took Cilla's shoulder, helping her up. She stood there, her knees weak from grief. I walked over to her father, staring into his eyes for a moment as if to apologize to what had happened to him. I reached over, grabbing his crown. I turned around to Cilla, her eyes swollen from tears. Those beautiful green eyes crowded with anguish. I walked over, grabbing her shoulder yet again. I raised it to her head. I looked into her eyes as I placed the crown atop her messy, unkempt hair.

We walked outside the palace together, her crown still atop her head. We found Herm and Nikolina awaiting our arrival.

"Have you seen everything you needed to see?" I asked.

"Yeah. That's the problem."

All four of us left together, heading towards the mountain. It was past the city, a little further north, next to a small town, one that was inhabited by actual living people.

Chapter 12: The City of Haze

It didn't take us long to get to Haze, the city that housed Mount Olympus. Arriving to the path leading into it we noticed it was rundown. Almost as if abandoned. The few citizens we did see were all weary, paranoid of outsiders. They hid behind their homes, peaking through the curtains. There was no food, there was no excitement inside this broken-down village. However, we weren't here to conversate with the locals, we just wanted to get up the Mountain and then back down.

Walking through the village, we were stopped by a boy in gray, no more than sixteen. He wore a chest piece of iron and wielded a worn-out steel blade to his side. His hair a dark blonde, and his eyes gray, matching the cloudy skies above.

"We don't have any money left. How much do you need?!" He shouted at us.

We looked at each other confused.

"You've got the wrong idea. We're not here for your money—"

"Then the food? We've got no more left. Not after your comrades and the beast atop the Mountain took it all!" He interrupted me, shouting yet again, pointing his blade towards us.

I approached the boy, gently moving Herm out of the way, "Listen. We're not here for anything of yours. We're not even sure of what's going on." I said as I looked to my circle.

The boy paused, sheathing his blade before asking,

"Who are you?"

"I'm Ollius. This is Nikolina, Cilla, and that's Hermaeus behind me. We're warriors wanting to speak with the Sage atop Mount Olympus."

"He's not taking any visitors right now. Leave the village at once." The boy ordered.

"That's not happening." I responded.

"Yes, it is." The boy said, once again wielding his blade.

"I promise you. You're not going to be able to stop me." I replied, grabbing my shield.

"Reach for your blade, rat. I won't let you plague this city anymore."

I smirked in response.

"Friends. This isn't getting us anywhere. Ollius, let it go." Herm chimed, holding me back.

"Friends? You don't even know my name. You walked into my city, ready to spread havoc, and expect me to shake your hand while doing it? Leave the city, now. I won't ask again." The man ordered, yet again.

"I don't appreciate your tone." I said pushing past Herm.

"Don't worry, you won't have to get used to it. Leave now." The boy said, getting into his stance.

I walked towards the boy as he swung.

I grabbed the edge of his blade, breaking it into two.

"We can either talk like adults so we may be able to help you, or I can send you flying into that house," I pointed at a deserted home to my right side, "and then get to climbing that mountain." My eyes lit up, sending fear through his bones.

The boy spoke, his voice clouded by the fear gripping his throat,

"You don't scare me—"

"Yes. Yes, I do." I interrupted.

Herm grabbed my shoulder pulling me away, stepping in.

"We're not here to hurt you. We want passage up the mountain, that's all."

The boy hesitated for a second,

"Fine. Just go." He collected his broken blade, running away, a tear dropping to his cheek.

"Hey! Where are you going?" Herm shouted after him.

Herm turned towards me, disappointed.

"What?" I asked.

"You didn't have to break his sword, Ollius. Look around you. This town doesn't have much. That blade was obviously very precious to him."

I scoffed as Herm, and the others walked away towards the mountain.

I let my blade loose of its sheath, striking it into the ground below.

Mount Olympus had a path ready to follow, so it was seemingly easy to climb. However, the distance itself was what made the ascension difficult. Mount Olympus was said to be the highest structure in Baylor, towering over any mountain that surrounds it. The tip could not be soon through the clouds it penetrated, and the weather would only get worse as you rose. Luckily, Thomas had told us to pack for the cold as he had once made the pilgrimage himself. He was crowned a captain of his own squadron before Sparta fell and was forced to climb the mountain to receive wisdom from the Sage.

Only a couple hours into the climb, my crew all felt the effects of the cold weather take command of our bones. Hermaeus was shivering, even past the thick robe he had brought with him. Cilla was using her dagger, the *Upbringing,* to keep her warm. Nikolina was surprisingly fine as she had doubled up on the thick robe the Legion provided. This would prove to be a very difficult venture, but it was one we had to make. It only got worse as when it got time to sleep through the night, the temperature dropped to freezing.

I was awake the whole night, protecting my Circle as sleep did not come easy to me that night. I kept the fire running as to provide a sanctuary for my squad. I was busy thinking about the people of Mizeria. Their deaths haunted me. Especially after today. The lives I took became something I grew to regret. Looking upon the destruction of Sparta, it hurt to think that I was capable of such destruction. I, the great Ollius, massacred armies of men, leaving children orphans, wives widowed, and sons vengeful—that was the simple truth and there was no getting past it. I rested my head on my pack, looking up into the sky. It was cold and filled with clouds. Snow piled all around the campfire. I heard scuffling on the other side of camp and raised my head to see. It was Cilla. She was standing up, heading towards some trees.

I rose up in response, as slow as I could, trying to make the least amount of noise. Where was she going so late at night? Was she hiding something?

She had her dagger to lighten the way for her as I followed based off the minimal amount of light provided by the Moon through the clouds.

She looked as if she was following something. Her movements were erratic, and she would constantly take sharp turns through the forest.

Left. Right. Left. Left.

She eventually did stop after a few minutes. I ducked behind a tree, trying to hide the glow from my crimson red eyes.

"Majestic." I heard across the distance.

I moved my head farther left to get a better look.

In front of me I saw a Pegasus. White wings, so extravagant and divine. Eyes of pure white, as if a pearl of the sea, and a body of gray as if summoned straight from the Underworld. The Pegasus was said to envelop the three domains of the Major Gods. A being that could not be imprisoned by one and was said to be a crime for the Gods to try.

The Pegasus neighed, alarming Cilla. It could sense me.

I dove down out of plain sight, looking under a log, my eyes shining a bright red yet again.

My red eyes almost cursed me, they made stealth a very difficult assignment. I couldn't see the Pegasus properly from the angle I was in, but I did see a bright light shine through the forest after Cilla laid her palm on it.

I decided to head back after taking another look to make sure Cilla was okay. I made my way back swiftly and took to staring at the sky yet again.

Cilla made her way back, noticing me.

"Ollius." She uttered, as her footsteps crunched in the snow.

"Cilla?" I asked, turning my head towards her.

"You followed me, didn't you?" She asked, crossing her arms.

"I don't like to lie, don't make me." I replied, smiling, and looking
towards the sky yet again.

She passed by me, finding a seat for herself nearby.

Some time passed as we both stared at the clouds, warming up by
the campfire.

"How did you do it Ollius?"

"Hmph?" I asked in response.

"For eighteen years, you were trapped in a pit—alone and angry.
You were lost, a child forgotten to history, because the common man
forgot you.

And yet, only a few feet away from me you lay, regretting what
you did to them. Haunted by those memories. In a way, it's almost as if
you're back in that cage." Cilla spoke, her voice soft and curious.

"Some days I feel like I never left." I continued,

"It took a lot of courage to leave. I was trapped, imprisoned even. But to escape means to know what the world outside consists of. I didn't know what trees were. I didn't know what grass was. I just dreamt of freedom—I didn't care what it would cost. I awoke every day to the same empty chamber, to the same sounds echoing the walls—to the same scent of sulfur blinding my smell. It became all I knew. When I was freed, I just wanted to explore the world. I wanted to breathe, I wanted to see, I wanted to hear, I wanted to smell, I just wanted to live. I didn't mean to hurt anyone, Ci. There was just this voice inside my head, begging me to. A rage, a primal instinct maybe. I could feel it wrap around me. It helped me cope with the loneliness. It helped me cope with the hate. It helped me cope with the loss of—" I stopped abruptly.

"Who? The loss of who?" Cilla pried, sitting up.

201

"It doesn't matter." I replied.

"Yes, it does. You know it does." She pressured.

"It wouldn't matter Ci." I interrupted.

"He's gone."

Cilla went to sleep not long after. I stayed awake, feeding the fire, and thinking. After I kill Hades and tear his head from his chest. I wanted to travel the world. I wanted to make stories of my own. Stories I could tell the next generation. Stories that would eternalize me in the stars. Ollius, the Gallant. Ollius, the Great. I didn't want to be the Beast of Baylor—it was a destiny that was forced upon me. I was tired of letting people decide anything for me. The Gods be damned—after I freed Sparta from the shackles of Hades, I would leave behind the Beast of Baylor—to make a new name for myself.

My circle awoke the next day, warm—thanks to my hard work. We packed up and made the trip up towards the Sage. We weren't far from our destination, only a couple hours to go before we were to meet face to face with the man that was capable of bringing me to Hades.

I spent time talking to Hermaeus while we climbed. He was a funny guy. He knew how, and when to make someone laugh. Safe to say, at this point, he was my best friend. I trusted him with my life, and with the life of others. If I were to pass before we completed this mission, I told him I wanted him to take over for me. I joked that I wanted him to become the next Beast of Baylor.

"That's impossible." He replied.

"What do you mean?"

"Ollius. If you were to die, I'd have no chance against whoever killed you." He chuckled as we shared a laugh.

We eventually did reach the Sage. After a long day and a half of climbing, we were exhausted.

Atop the mountain stood a home. It was a single story and was built of stone and wood. Hermaeus pointed out it must have been built up of a very strong foundation to have survived this long up against this kind of wind.

I took the first step towards the door as the others followed. I held my sheathe under my robe in preparation, forgetting I had let my blade go back at Haze.

I swung the door open as we all dove in, covering all three directions.

My Circle stood at the entrance as I walked in to find an empty home. Bookshelves filled with books, some having to be stacked on top. To my right I saw the living room, empty and lifeless besides the spiders swinging a new web. To my left I saw the kitchen, cabinets of wood, and tables of the same. It looked to be abandoned.

I looked towards my crew, signaling them to stay.

I took a walk around the house, heading towards a dark room in the corner of the house past the kitchen.

As I walked into the darkness, I felt the room grow cold.

"Ollius."

I grabbed my sheath to no avail jumping back to find the entrance was gone. I stood in a dark abyss, the light from my eyes fighting the shadows enveloping me.

"Where am I? Who are you? Where is the Sage? How do you know who I am?" I questioned, looking around for the voice.

"One question at a time, Son of Sparta."

I paused before asking, "Who are you?"

The voice, shriveled and old spoke back,

"I am the Sage."

I took a breath of relief, my guard still up.

"Where are you?" I asked into the darkness.

"I am no longer in your realm, Ollius." He spoke back, a sort of wisdom guiding his voice.

"You mean, you died?" I asked, letting go of the iron grip I held.

"Every race has a finish line, Son of Sparta. Even yours."

"Where am I?" I continued asking, ignoring his warning.

"I don't care to know, Ollius. This is merely a way for us to communicate." He answered swiftly.

"How do you know who I am?"

"The heart of man. The pride of God. Eyes of a pure rage. Who else but you Ollius?" The Sage replied.

"You know me then. You must know why I'm here!" I shouted, pausing before continuing, "I need a way to the Underworld! I need a way to Hades!" I shouted to the abyss.

"For what reason, Son of Sparta?" His voice rose from the shadows.

"So, I may put an end to his pathetic way of life." I replied.

"So, the cycle of hate continues. Tell me, Spartan. For the act of massacring the men of Mizeria, do you wield any regret?" He asked.

"That's different. They didn't take Nikolaus!" I shouted.

"Yet they took Dimitris." He replied.

"Don't you dare bring up Dimitris!" I interrupted.

"The countless lives you took that night were innocent. Whether you believe it or not, you were the Dragon that took Nikolaus at one point. If you wish to avenge your fallen, that's fine—but don't dare plead innocent. You are a monster." He paused before he continued,

"I am no longer of your realm. I have left Baylor long ago. The day Sparta fell, they took me too. I understand your hate, I understand your pain. I have lived hundreds of lifetimes. I have witnessed plague, I have witnessed famine, I have witnessed greed.

However, none compared to war. War takes the guilty, the innocent, and everything in between. With plague, famine, greed, there is always a cure, a solution, and envy. With war, there's always another—because someone's always losing. You are free to your own choices Ollius. I just want to make sure you know the consequences. When you kill Hades, the wrath of the Gods will be unleashed. You will suffer. She will suffer. Sparta will bear witness to the death of a God. There is much you don't know Spartan." The Sage warned.

I paused before I looked up towards the darkness. My eyes, shining brighter.

"If killing Hades is a mistake. Then at least I'll finally be able to make one of my own."

"What choice do I have Sage?" I continued, "With all your wisdom, I ask you! If Hades lives, my people cannot! He will attack us again! If he lives, I'll be forced to mourn my comrades' day after day! If I grow to regret this, then at least only I will. Let me make that sacrifice! Let me suffer so my friends must not!" I shouted into the darkness yet again.

"You won't suffer alone. You will drag down the mortal world alongside you. Men, women, children of Baylor will be slaughtered by the thousands! You will start a war you cannot win! If Baylor suffers—it will be by the Gods hands, but you will be the reason. Hades' death will mean the end of mortal life. I know your heart, Ollius. You will grow to regret this—that I can promise. Knowing this, I won't give you the information you seek until you admit the truth! The death of Hades is not for Sparta, it's for your own selfish desire! It's to soothe the aching crave inside your heart every waking moment; to shed blood; to shed tears; to tear apart worlds!" The Sage shouted. A moment of silence following his lecture.

"A leviathan. A monster. They were right to call you a beast." He continued as I fell to my knees. A weight of insurmountable strength piled atop me.

"If it were up to me, you would answer for your crimes. I'd leave you to suffer here, fighting against your sanity for hundreds of years. You are a danger to the mortal world. You are a traitor of reason. You are the monstrosity of Mizeria. You were bred to hate. You were bred to kill. Your father was the same. That's why the Greek world rid of him." The Sage spoke, angering me.

"You don't know me." I replied, fighting against the pressure he invoked.

"You'd be surprised—"

"And you'd be wrong." I interrupted, breaking free from his grip.

"If I'm a monster, then so be it." A silence preluded, "I am who I am. No God can take that from me. I don't care how strong they are. I don't care how right they are. I've always been me. Call me a beast, call me a Spartan—I don't care. At the end of the day, I'm the only one that knows who I am. I'm the only one who should. If I'm a monster, then so be it!" I shouted as my eyes flamed a crimson red.

"I'll never let anyone control me. I've fought too hard to find who I am. I don't need you to speak for me, Sage. I don't need you tell me the future. I'll decide!"

"You're just like your father. Arrogant, yet could compel any mortal he met."

Pausing before he continued, "To gain entrance to the Underworld, you must ask Hades himself." He finally answered my question.

"You're kidding." I said, feeling hopeless.

"I didn't come this far for your jokes Sage. Hades would never let me inside his realm, he knows I'm out for his head after what he did to the Legion."

"Not necessarily, Son of Sparta. Within the Underworld, Hades controls all. His will lives through every fabric of the realm. He only sent the Dragon to kill you. He has no problem inviting you into the Lion's den, matter of fact, he planned to all along. You must offer a sacrifice, and an artifact blessed by the Gods to contact Hades. In a forest not far from the City of Lonz lies the Hellflame—a blade once wielded by the son of Hades. Afterwards, head far back to where you met the Skip. He can lead you to a beast that wields a Godly Artifact within its eye."

"The Skip?" I asked, puzzled.

"He's not come to be known as that yet, I understand. To you, you know him as Triton, the Boy of the Sea."

I stood shocked; how did the Sage know about Tri?

"That's all I need." I replied.

"There's not much more I can tell you—not that you'd listen. For the first and last time, goodbye Son of Sparta." His voice rose, as a vortex of shadows grew around me.

I was pulled into it, cycling around in a circle before I was thrown through the door I had entered from, breaking through the walls of the old wooden home.

I pulled myself up from the cliff I had dug my fingers into. Below me was a height of which I could not survive. Mount Olympus stood at the peak of Baylor, so below me was not only a terrifying height, but everything and anything man has done, didn't try, or ever could do. Looking up, I saw a lone rose sitting idly by, surrounded by snow—almost as if taunting me. I could lose my life at a moment's notice, and there was not a thing I could do to stop it.

Herm ran out to meet me, the others following not long after.

"Ollius! Are you okay?" He shouted as he closed in.

"I'm fine." I paused, "I'm fine."

Chapter 13: The Cyclops

Herm helped me to my feet as we stood staring at the cabin being enveloped by fog. Before our very eyes, it was disappearing.

"No! No! This can't be happening!" Herm shouted as the cabin disappeared.

"It's fine. I have the answers we were after." I announced, placing my hand on his shoulder.

"No! I left my backpack in there!" Herm shouted back at me as we all shared a laugh.

As we made our way down the mountain, I decided to break the bad news to them. We were exhausted, pushed to our limits. The snow began stacking a couple feet thick.

"The Sage told me how to get to the Underworld—and it's insane."

"Whether it's a lava moat, a ship full of snakes, or even a mountain taller than this one. We'll follow you till the ends of the Earth, Ollius." Herm spoke.

"That's the problem, Herm. I am giving you guys one last chance to leave. The Sage told me; I'd grow to regret this decision—that everyone around me will grow to regret this decision. The death of Hades will be felt on a global scale. I need to make sure you guys understand that it's okay if you need to leave."

There was a silence as we walked the path.

"Hades' Dragon slaughtered a lot of good men. I don't care what it takes." Herm replied.

"He took my brother." Nikolina chimed in.

"He's hurt my people." Cilla spoke, breaking her quiet streak.

"There is much work to do then." I stopped, pulling a map out of my backpack, "We must head to Lonz. He told me to find Hellflame—a blade once wielded by the Son of Hades. Now—it's our way into the Underworld."

"How are we supposed to use that to get into the Underworld?" Nikolina asked.

"It alongside a God Artifact presents us an opportunity to speak with Hades. From there—we have to convince him to let us in."

"What?!" Shouted all three of them.

"It's the only way to enter the Underworld. We need his permission."

"There's no way he'll let us in—he knows we're after his head." Nikolina said, crossing her arms.

"The Sage seems to think this was actually Hades' plan all along."

"Then it's a trap!" Herm hollered.

"It is—but what choice do we have? What can we do?" I asked the group, "Does anyone else have any ideas? I guess we should wait for Hades to send another Dragon to destroy the fortress!"

"No one's saying that—"

"If Sparta falls—I have no home Herm. I have to fight. I have to do whatever it takes. For Sparta to live, I am willing to die. If you're too afraid, I'll gladly walk into the lion's den on my own."

There was a silence before I continued,

"If that means diving into a trap head on, I have to do it. I will not stand idly by as my people are sent to their death to battle a flame wielding Dragon again. This is Sparta's last stand. If you are not willing to join me in this battle, I understand, no hard feelings. But don't you dare try to stop me." I lectured, walking past them.

We continued to walk down the mountain. The snow piled on, making it harder to venture through. Our legs grew weary, and the cold only got worse.

It didn't take long for trouble to find itself in our grasp.

I noticed a cave on the path. It was empty and looked to be safe. My crew was exhausted and needed a place to rest. We set up camp in there, preparing a campfire to fight the cold with.

Earlier on our venture down, we caught some game in the form of a small rabbit—since Herm left his backpack in the cabin when it disappeared, we were low on rations. We had no choice but to cook it up and share it four ways.

The snow had a sort of beauty in it. As I stood inside the cave, leaning towards the right side admiring the blanket of white that kept building up, I found myself mesmerized. It was my first experience with snow—and true cold. I could feel my eyes fail to stay awake. I had been up for too long, and my body was exhausted.

A few hours into our stay, I noticed the snow slowly die down outside,

"I think tomorrow will be an easier descent. The snow is quieting."

"Good. I feel as if my ears are going to freeze off." Spoke Herm.

I chuckled.

We had all closed our eyes, especially me. Hermaeus had offered to stay up and keep the fire running for us—but after he had spent over an hour trying to start the fire just to fail miserably and have

Nikolina start it in one spark, we had all decided to let Nikolina take tonight.

I slept wonderfully. It was warm, quiet, and I felt cozy and safe. As I had closed my eyes to join the world of dreams and wonder, I felt the cold air slowly invite itself inside. A perfect combination—a frosty warmth as one might call it. My fingers finally warm, and my thick fur robe enveloping me in an embrace. The campfire burning in the background as if two swords clashed. As I relaxed an exhale, I heard a distant sound. Maybe an animal of sorts? I heard it cry through the Mountain, its sound bouncing off every tree and stone in its way. Majestic and violent it soared through the woods.

Tap. Tap. Tap. I heard.

It only got louder as my ears naturally pressed to the ground. A reflex and consequence of a peaceful sleep.

Boom. Boom. Boom. The ground shook as it dashed gracefully.

As I had finally escaped to the world of dreams—I was abruptly shaken awake.

I opened my eyes as Nikolina stared into mine shouting.

"Ollius, let mup!" She screamed; the only thing visible to my fleeting eyes were hers.

"What?" I said, sleep deprived and aching to close my eyes again.

"Ollius!" Suddenly, the outside world pulled me from my half-slumber, sounds and the background shot into view. I was awake again.

"Get up!" She hollered as I finally understood.

"Somethings coming—and fast!" Herm shouted, his sword already unsheathed.

I stood up, now fully aware of the situation. That graceful sound I was admiring was the sound of death marching towards us.

Cilla wielded her blade of light, as Nikolina stood back.

I grabbed my shield walking towards the entrance.

"Ollius! Where are you going?!" Herm asked, shouting.

"To meet it." I said, not halting my venture into the unknown.

As I approached the exit of the cave, I saw the monster the townspeople—well townsperson, spoke of. It was tall and had some weight to it. It stood easily twelve, maybe thirteen feet tall. It had one eye, and its teeth decayed. Bald, and angry, it stared at me. That's when I realized, this was probably its home.

"Can I help you?" I asked, my shield to my side.

"Me. Home." It fought to answer back against a very thick language barrier.

"This is your home?" I asked.

"Me! Home!" It shouted this time, pointing its gigantic wooden club to the cave behind me.

"I understand. This is your home." I said, raising my arms in surrender.

"Leave! Leave Mama!" It hollered.

"We just need to stay the night—it's really cold outside—"

"Leave! Mama!" It shouted as it ran towards me, swinging its club down.

I blocked its attack with my shield, forcing it to the side, I jumped back.

All I wanted to do was tear its arms off so I can finally go back to sleep—but I knew that would only end in meaningless bloodshed—there was a better way to deal with this.

"Just calm down—we'll leave."

"Leave! Me! Home!" It cried yet again.

Herm and Cilla came out to meet me, the creature now standing in front of the cave.

I gestured Herm to not attack.

"Ollius! Do you need help?"

"No! I think its mother is in the cave!" I shouted back, realizing I no longer had a blade to defend myself with.

The Cyclops growled, throwing its wooden club to the side.

As it attacked again, I dodged, landing a punch to its gut, sending it to its knees.

It shot up, picking me up and tackling me into a nearby gigantic tree—chipping it.

The creature stared into my eyes letting out a roar. It's disgusting saliva drenching me, only making my cold exhausted body weaker.

Before it had the chance of pounding me with its gigantic fist, I slid beneath it. The tree broke from its stump, falling towards me and the Cyclops—landing atop the monster and knocking it out.

I laid a few feet in front of the Cyclops, holding up the colossal tree for dear life. With all my might, I tossed it to the side. Herm ran to me, helping me up. I felt a soreness in my left knee that I couldn't explain.

"Just one night. I just want to fall asleep for one night." I said falling down to my weak knee from a lack of proper sleep and nourishment. Herm grabbed me walking me back to the cave.

I breathed heavily, exhausted, hungry, and sleepy.

The Cyclops had been defeated, but our night would only prove to get worse.

We had strapped it to the cave, nailing in stakes to the wall.

"This must be the monster the kid spoke of." Herm sighed.

"So, no one thought to check the cave?" Cilla scolded.

"It's freezing out there, Ci. I was exhausted—you can't pin this on me."

"I'm still going to." She said, clearly upset.

224

I exhaled a breath of irritancy. I reached down towards my boot, grabbing a dagger.

"You guys stay here—make sure he can't get out of that." I ordered as I pointed a torch towards the campfire, lighting it.

"Where are you going?" Nikolina spoke up.

"To meet our host."

"With your knee in that shape?" Herm chimed in.

"I'll be fine. Don't worry."

I took the first of many steps deeper inwards.

Even with the torch lighting my way—I found it still too dark to navigate, which got me thinking about how the Cyclops could survive here. It was freezing outside, and there were barely any animals that he could survive on. On top of everything else, he was providing for his mother. This was sketchy—I had a bad feeling.

As I wandered into the unknown, I could only hear the sound of my own heartbeat pulsing louder than the pain in my knee. The quiet got me thinking about this trial. I was to face Hades very soon. The God of the Underworld, feared by men and Gods the same. I had no clue to his strength or abilities, or even his home. Was I in over my head? Am I right to endanger my crew's lives for this? I could spend day in and day out trying to convince myself that I'm doing this for the greater good of Sparta but truth be told, I was only doing this to avenge Nikolaus. I know that now. His final words haunted me every day.

As I ventured deeper, I heard a voice behind me.

"Interloper." The voice, soft and feminine.

I turned around with haste shouting,

"Where are you?!" I proceeded to mumble under my breath, "I'm getting sick of people sneaking up on me like this."

"Bold of you to ask, seeing as you're in my home." The voice spoke back.

"You are in danger." It continued as wind soar through, tossing my torch away, the fire ceasing.

"I don't take kindly to threats." I said, looking back in front of me.

I felt something warm and thick wrap around me. My legs, my arms, my chest. I was trapped all around.

"What're you doing to me? Let me go!" I shouted, fighting back against the vines tightening my grasp.

"You should be afraid; I know exactly what you are." The voice warned.

"You know what I am? Then you should know better than to attack me like this."

It chuckled—its voice echoing.

"If you knew who I am, you would not be speaking so highly of yourself. You are in my domain after all." The woman spoke back, its grip tightening.

I grunted, fighting back as my arm got loose,

"When I get out of here, I'm going to slice your son's throat and drag his lifeless body to see you for the final time!" I shouted as I got my other arm loose.

"You will do no such thing!" I felt a force push me back towards the wall as the cave collapsed atop me. I heard her scream and shout obscenities through the debris. It was cold, the bitter taste of dirt and stone laid on my tongue.

"I know your kind! You plague this world, and for that I cannot forgive you." The woman spoke, as a light erupted deeper in the cave.

A scream shot the debris off me as a vine carried me up from my throat.

"You Gods will suffer. All of you." I said, fighting through strained breaths.

"Gods? You think I'm a God?!" The woman shouted.

"Don't compare me to those traitors." She continued.

"Let me go, or you will force my hand." I warned, as I grabbed the vine, tearing it off my neck little by little.

"Do your worst."

I grew angry, reaching for the vine and tearing it off as my crimson rage lit up the dark cave.

"How much are you going to take before you're satisfied?!" The woman shouted before I got a chance to attack.

"What?"

"You've taken my son, thrown my husband to the pit of Tartarus, and destroyed my kingdom all in a venture for power. I never forgot. I will never forget—I can't forget. The pain has marked me for eternity! I ask you again, Son of Olympus, how much more?!" The woman pleaded, shrieking through the cave. A burst of wind threw me back towards the exit. I drove my hand through the wall fighting against the pressure.

"I have no idea what you're talking about! I didn't come here to fight!" I shouted back, as the shriek's wind only increased.

"Leave my home!" Her voice multiplied, as if coming by many sources.

"Enough!" I shouted, my eyes glow intensifying as I dug my foot into the ground taking my first step.

"How? How are you still fighting?! Who are you?!" She shouted as the wind increased tenfold.

I shouted, forcing my feet to take another step.

The wind tore through my robe. A pressure unlike anything I've ever experienced.

I squatted down, getting ready for a leap as my anger swelled.

"Your name. I need your name!" The woman hollered, pain wrapping her words in a cold blanket of anguish.

My pace only grew quicker as I left debris in my trace. Mere steps turned into a full sprint.

I landed a punch square into the woman's face, knocking her into the wall behind her.

I stood over her, the wind finally ceased. I could hear her struggle to breathe.

Out of breath and out of patience I looked down to face the woman.

The woman sat up, her hair an ivy green. The only noticeable feature I could see in the dim light my eyes provided.

"How much more Son of Olympus?"

"How much more? What're you talking about? I didn't come here to fight. I came here to ask you to stop sending your son to terrorize the village."

"He's not terrorizing them! He's just different— so they treat him differently. He's different, so to them he's a monster!"

I was silent for a second.

"You don't know what it's like. He's known nothing but loneliness his entire life. He has no brother, no sister. I am his only kin. Do you wish to take me away from him too?" The woman said, tears enveloping her words.

"You're strong! Isn't that enough for you?! Must you prove it by tearing everything I have left away from me?!" The woman continued to cry.

I knew what that was like. That loneliness could kill. The town feared his strength, as Mizeria feared mine. Here was a woman merely trying to protect her son. She reminded me of Dimitris, and I knew he'd be disappointed if he were to see me now.

"I'm sorry."

A silence preluded,

"What?"

"I'm sorry."

"You're apologizing?"

"I know what that persecution is like, and for that I'm sorry." I offered my hand to her.

"I've never heard an Olympian apologize for anything." She said, taking my hand and standing up.

"An Olympian?" I asked as she rose a plant from the ground below, lighting up the cave.

I could now see the woman clearly. She was shorter than me, her eyes almost unnaturally green. She wore a piece of cloth that surrounded her body like a dress. Her skin was youthful but told stories of hundreds of years.

Alongside the woman, I saw the end of the cave. It was a room, furnished with a bed, a table, and other necessities.

"You can't fool me; I can see everything."

"What do you mean? What's an Olympian?"

"You mean you don't know?" She asked, not trusting of my word.

"What don't I know?"

"Have you ever wondered why you're capable of such strength, Son of Olympus?" She asked as she walked away towards her bed.

"No, now that you mention it."

"You are capable of great power. Your rage strengthens you, but your eyes blind you. You know that. With power always comes sacrifice." She lectured.

"Who are you?" I asked.

"I go by many names. Mother to my son, Queen to my husband. Gaia of the Titans."

"The Titans? You're a Titan?" I found this hard to believe.

"I know what it sounds like, but I only ask for the benefit of your doubt.

Zeus betrayed us. My brothers and sisters died at his hand. The Titans collapsed the day Zeus took over our land. We created him—we created all of you. We loved the Mortals. When Zeus, and the Gods took over our land, they brought the monsters you see today alongside them. To give themselves a purpose. In return for the Mortals' everlasting servitude, they protected them from monsters of their own creation. Zeus plagued the sky, Poseidon plagued the sea, and Hades created the Underworld. I survived the onslaught, but because of Zeus' position atop Olympus, I can never leave this cave without being spotted. I am cursed to stay here, stuck inside this cave. So close to who I used to be, and yet so far."

I was silent, not sure of how to reply.

"Past the hatred, the contempt, bitter feeling of anger, the swelling desire for vengeance—I see good. You remind me so much of someone I used to know."

"Then you know." I chimed in.

"I don't, but I see everything. Right now, I see a child. Lost, confused, angry." She paused, "Grieving."

"Don't let your anger win, Olympian. It's your greatest strength—but it's also your greatest weakness."

"I don't need a lecture, Gaia."

"You can't fool me."

"Enough. I'll help your son. As long as you can get him to behave."

I walked off.

I heard her smirk before I made my way towards the entrance of the cave.

Arriving, I saw the Cyclops awake and raging at my crew.

Herm had his blade to the Cyclops neck, shouting at the beast to calm down.

"Herm! Put your blade down!" I ordered.

"Ollius?" He turned his head towards me.

"Put it down!"

The Cyclops grew quiet as I approached him.

"What's your name?" I asked.

The Cyclops gurgled his saliva, its' residue hitting my face,

"Phemus!"

"How would you like to make some friends, Phemus?" I asked, wiping my face off with a nearby shirt, as he returned a smile.

"Your mother told me everything. You'll be fine."

I grabbed a dagger from my boot cutting his restraints.

The Cyclops stood up as Cilla and Hermaeus prepared for a fight that never came.

"Don't." I ordered as Phemus made his way towards the exit of the cave.

"What's going on?" Herm asked.

"A lot. I met his mother, and this next part will be difficult for you to believe."

"Was she nice?" Nikolina chimed in.

"Oh no. She tried to kill me—multiple times."

"Dude, what happened in there?" Herm questioned.

"She collapsed the tunnel atop me—even pummeled me for a bit—but she finally got it through to me that her son just wants some friends."

"I knew it." Herm interrupted.

"No, you didn't." Nikolina chimed in.

"There is also the matter that she is Gaia of the Titans." I returned.

"The Titans? As in Olympus' predecessors?" Herm beamed.

"Yeah. Those Titans."

Before Hermaeus got a chance to speak, I interrupted, "Listen. I don't want to talk about this anymore. We need to get to Lonz, and from there to Kavala. We have work to do—let's not dwell on this any longer."

Herm said nothing, holstering his longsword behind his back before taking off down the mountain.

I followed after grabbing my pack.

We made our way down the mountain with Phemus alongside us. The last couple of hours of the descent flew by as we took turns atop Phemus' shoulder.

Reaching the broken-down town of Haze, we found it abandoned yet again.

"How are we supposed to announce anything with them hiding?" Herm asked.

"I've got an idea." I said as I walked to the center of their very small town.

"Citizens of Haze! I ask you to leave your homes as I have brought you salvation!" I shouted at the top of my lungs.

The boy from before, now wielding my blade, awoke from behind a home.

"What do you want?" He asked.

"Your name, to start."

The kid scoffed, "Alexander. I'm the Guardian of the village."

"Guardian?" Herm asked.

"I'm the only one left that gives a damn. We don't have much left. I provide for the elderly and the weak. Whatever you want, we don't have."

"We're merely here to help, Alexander. What about us seems so menacing?" I asked.

"You mean other than the thirteen-foot behemoth behind you?"

The cyclops roared in response as Herm held it back.

"It means no harm. I promise you."

"It's been stealing our food for months!"

"It doesn't know any better. His name is Phemus. He's here to make your acquaintance."

"We're not interested. He's a freak! My people would never accept him."

"Don't you dare speak to him that way." My voice rose as I stepped towards Alexander,

"I have been more than pleasant to you Alexander. Half the men that had the regret of meeting me didn't manage to let out a single sentence. To judge off a glimpse is unforgivable. I won't stand for it. You call yourself a Guardian, yet you turn your back on the one that needs you the most."

"You don't get to speak to me that way! You don't understand what we've lost!" Alexander argued.

"I understand Alexander, because I'm usually the one that takes!" I shouted,

"Give him a chance. He can save your pitiful town." I said as I turned around towards Phemus.

"Trust me. Knowing who his mother is, if he really wanted you gone, this town would be nothing but ashes by now." I looked back at Alexander.

The kid sighed, placing his arms on his hips, "I'll have to talk with the families here. It's up to them if they're comfortable with him staying." The kid leapt around heading towards one of the homes.

"Alexander." I halted him.

"Yes?"

"You have the makings of a leader, boy. Don't let your personal issues get in the way of making the right choice. The riskiest choice you can make is not to take one at all."

"Risk is for the hopeful, Ollius." Alexander walked off.

I turned around to see Herm and the rest of the crew staring at me.

"What?"

"I like this side of you." Herm spoke up.

"Shut up."

"No seriously, you've grown." Herm offered his hand as I blew past it.

I walked past Herm to reach Phemus,

"Go ahead and grab it. We'll wait down here."

The cyclops hurried up the mountain as I turned around to greet Alexander yet again.

"I talked to my elders. They're willing to give him a chance as long as he doesn't steal our food anymore."

"Oh, he'll do a lot more than that," I said as I pointed towards the entrance of the mountain.

Descending the mountain was Phemus, the Cyclops, carrying a dead moose carcass in his arms.

"He's brought dinner."

The cyclops dropped the corpse in front of Alex and extended an arm towards him. Alexander, upon hesitation, shook it, although his entire arm was enveloped within the Cyclops palm. From that handshake bred a friendship between the Cyclops and the Town of Haze. In the coming years, I learned the Cyclops was a big part in what built Haze to become the superpower it became.

We left Haze in capable hands. Not only did they have a Cyclops to protect their land, but a Titan in the shadows. Our next venture would prove to be long and tedious still. We had to recover the Hellflame, through any means necessary.

Through Lonz we find the forest the Sage spoke of.

Chapter 14: Depths of Hell

We walked for days, Lonz being a fair distance away from Haze. During that time, Herm found every opportunity to make us laugh, but I was too far concerned with the next challenge to crack a smile. I found I didn't have many stories besides the ones I made with the Legion. The only other ones I could think of hurt too much. Dimitris was still a sore subject for me.

It's a crazy thing to think about but tragedy finds a way to bring people together. We all had our fair share of misfortune growing up, so it was easier to trust one another. Nikolina grew up with the sole purpose to escape her brother's shadow, just to find it was far too bright to venture from the safety of her twin's contour. Cilla was raised with hopes of taking over the helm, a pressure that seemed to occupy every waking moment of her life. Hermaeus was alone growing up, spending every night sleeping in the school, and every day on the training grounds looking for a fight. He had to grow strong, he didn't have a choice. That longsword was the only thing Thomas could grab in his father's final moments. None of that mattered when we all stood alongside each other as equals. We don't care where we came because although we all suffered in different quantities, it was because of the same calamity—the same night that marked us with an eternal lust for freedom. There was a reason Thomas put the four of us together, and I finally understood what it was. It was because of all the soldiers and talent at camp, we were the only ones that could understand each other.

Our provisions now gone, we had to resort to hunting game along the way, which took time we didn't have. But it was thanks to this that we finally had the answers to what Lina and Herm were.

Throughout our adventures, Hermaeus would always find himself to her side. We all had an inkling that he did like her, and when you live a life like this one, it can be taken away very quickly. We have to learn to live in the now, because if we don't, we risk losing a chance to live at all.

It was late at night, and we had settled in for another night of camping in the wilderness. Herm and I were awake, sitting around the campfire, coming up with a strategy to get the Hellflame.

"I'm telling you; our best bet is force. You're strong, Cilla's fast, I've got guts, Lina's smart, we should take advantage of our strengths."

"There might be a better way."

"It's a dangerous precedent Ollius. If we give up the element of surprise, we risk losing our comrades."

"You know I won't let that happen." I said, interrupting him.

Hermaeus sighed, looking over to his side at Lina who was sound asleep.

"You like her." I spoke abruptly.

"I might."

"You should say something—"

"I can't. She's dealing with a lot right now. I can't pour that on her."

"I think it might actually help." I replied, locking my palms atop my knee.

"How? She just lost her brother Ollius."

"Exactly. She's alone right now. I'm not saying you should date her, or even try anything. It'd just be nice for her to know she's not alone. She lost a piece of herself that day, Herm. I think she'd feel better knowing someone has her back again."

Hermaeus was silent before he spoke, "Maybe you're right."

"I always am. I'm surprised you don't know this." I laughed as I got up to throw wood into the fire.

"I wouldn't say always." He smirked.

"Watch your tongue, heathen." I joked.

Hermaeus continued laughing, as he looked over at Lina. She slept quietly, and I could tell he wanted nothing more than to put his arm around her.

I sat back down after nurturing the fire.

I looked into the sky. Swarming with stars. A beautiful sight to behold.

I felt sour.

So many nights I spent staring into the sky for an answer to a question I never bothered to ask. That's when I realized, it wasn't the answer I was looking for. It was the question.

Who am I?

I've heard I was a Son of Olympus. I've been told I was a Spartan. Some even called me a beast. So many names, but none of them were mine. A name is powerful—from it, we decide whether or not to trust, to love, or even to hate. A name becomes our identity. It's who we are—and it's the one thing out of our control that we accept.

So, who am I? I wasn't even sure Ollius was mine. It was something Dimitris decided for me. My father's gone, and my mother—I wouldn't even know where to begin.

"Ollius, grab me the wine from your pack."

"Why? You know for a fact you can't hold your liquor."

"I totally can. I outdrank Sterg the other night."

"No. You didn't." I said as I reached for my pack.

"You don't know what you don't know." Herm said as I rolled my eyes and dug inside.

I felt something. It was a cold piece of cloth.

I raised my eyebrow and looked at Herm. I left Dimitris' cloth back at home, what could this be?

"What?" He asked.

"I don't know." I said as I pulled the cold strip of cloth out.

"Ollius. When did you grab that?!" Herm shouted as he stood up.

"I didn't. I just found it in my pack!"

"Stuff doesn't just show up in your pack! Someone put it there!"

"I don't know who! Stop shouting!"

Lina rubbed her eyes waking up slowly,

"What's going on?" She asked as Cilla awoke from the other side of the campfire.

"It's the robe! The robe is in Ollius' pack!"

"That can't be," She yawned, "Didn't he lose that back at Kavala?"

"Yeah. That's what I thought too. I mean, we must've been mistaken. There's no other way." I explained as I stared mindlessly at the dark robe that sat on my lap.

"No way. Matullus would've sensed it in a heartbeat." Lina, now fully awake, said.

"Then how did it get in my pack?"

"I put it there." A voice rose mere feet away from the campfire. The darkness of the cloudy night protecting the speaker.

I stood up, grabbing a small blade that rested at my side.

My crew did the same, arming themselves with whatever they could. I felt the heat of Cilla's *Upbringing* behind me, giving me a sense of urgency.

It was silent, before I asked into the dark,

"Who's there?"

"Aren't you sick and tired of asking that question, Ollius? How many times have you found yourself in this situation?" An unfamiliar, and feminine voice answered, wielding an aggressive tone.

"Too many times to count. Show yourself."

"I don't have to do anything."

"Then you'll reap what you sow." I declared.

"You talk big. I like that."

"Show yourself. This is your final warning." I threatened, gripping the dagger.

The voice laughed abruptly as a foot stepped into the light.

I put my dagger up, pointing it towards her.

Out from the shadows a black-haired raven introduced herself. She was short, kind of attractive, and had two bright yellow blazing suns for eyes. They were glowing, just as mine do.

"What do you want? Why did you put the robe in my pack?" I asked, breaking the awkward silence.

"If I didn't, you'd never believe me to be who I am."

"And who might that be?" Herm asked.

"Quiet, dog. The men are talking." She scolded.

"You'll not speak to Herm that way."

"I don't like him. I'll speak to him as I see fit." She said as she got closer to me,

"Don't take another step, I don't trust you." I raised the dagger to her neck.

"I wouldn't either."

"Who are you?" I asked, pressuring the dagger upon her.

"Melanie. I'm the daughter of Hades."

"You're what?"

"I told you. I'm Melanie, the daughter of Hades."

My eyes burst a crimson red light yet again. I grabbed Melanie's collar, ready to send Hades a message. I felt an unusual urge to look behind me towards Cilla. Her eyes begged me to stop.

I took a step back, lowering my dagger,

"What do you want?"

"The same thing you do." She said as she fixed her shirt, "To kill my father."

"You've got to be kidding, we're not going to trust you!" Herm hollered from behind me.

"What did I say about speaking, you overgrown mutt!?" Melanie screamed back at him.

"Disrespect him again and I'll send you back to your father—and he's right, we can't trust you."

"I'll speak to him however I wish to, and I don't care if you trust me. I trust you. I can't tell you the reason why, yet. But in due time, you'll come to understand your place in Olympus." She lectured.

"My place in Olympus? My place is here, in Baylor. Fighting alongside the Legion."

"That's not for you to decide, Son of Sparta."

"Nothing's been decided—and if it has, there's not a single being strong enough to force me to comply."

"That's where we disagree. You truly have no idea what's out there. It's a moot point; you've got to leave for Kavala—now."

"I don't have to do anything. Plus, we've still got to find the Hellflame. Lonz is first."

"No. You don't. You've already got it."

"What do you mean?" Herm asked, beaming at the thought of annoying her.

Melanie sighed, directing our attention towards the robe.

"There it is."

"You mean inside it?" I asked.

"No. The robe. That's the Hellflame." She answered, with a tone insinuating I should've already known that.

"I don't know what you mean. That's not a blade Melanie. That's a robe."

"You're telling me you were on your way to Lonz to search an entire forest for a blade without knowing anything about it?"

"Well, we know it belongs to Hades' son."

"Hades doesn't have a son you dimwit."

"But the Sage—"

"I don't care what that old man said. I'm telling you; Hades doesn't have a son. The Hellflame's mine. It's always been mine."

There was a moment of silence before I asked,

"The Sage is all knowing. How could he get it so wrong?"

"Honestly, you look at a lot of the stories and most of them are pretty misogynistic. They don't believe the all-powerful Hades, God of the Underworld, could bear only daughters. I promise you; I don't have a brother."

"Whatever. How does the Hellflame work?" I asked, reaching down to grab it.

"The Hellflame doesn't 'work'—it's not an item, or a tool. It's quite literally the embodiment of fire and death. I took it from the Underworld a long time ago, and my father's been after it since. I'm not exactly sure why."

"You know we plan on giving this back to Hades, right?"

"If it means you put an end to his reign, I'm okay with that." She declared, crossing her arms.

"What did he do to you? Why do you want him gone so bad?" I asked.

"He didn't do anything to me, but my fathers a monster. That I can promise you."

"I want you to tell me why. I might even let you come along."

"I'm no warrior, Ollius. I just want my father to suffer."

"Why?"

"I can't sit around and let him torment my mother for a moment longer. He trapped her there, forcing her to become the Queen of the Underworld against the wishes of my grandmother. She can never leave, and she's tormented by that fact every day."

I looked around to see my crew stare back at me, awaiting an answer I had yet to conclude.

"If I kill Hades. Your mother will still be trapped. I know of the tale. The pomegranate that trapped her there for eternity."

"It's funny. Before Hades, pomegranate was actually mother's favorite fruit. It was fitting that it was her end.

You don't know this, so I shouldn't be surprised. But marriages work differently in the realm of the Gods. When Hades dies, Persephone, my mother, will be the next to rule the Underworld. After her, her eldest daughter, and then I. When Persephone becomes the ruler of the Underworld, she's allowed to make changes. The seal is not a curse, it's a feature. A perk of becoming one of the three most powerful Gods."

I scoffed,

"How do I know you're not leading me to a trap?"

"I have nothing to gain. My father has tormented many souls, but none as worse as my mothers. I beg of you, Son of Sparta. Free my mother. End Hades' reign, and I shall grant you anything you desire."

There was silence.

"I had already had plans to trophy Hades' head long before you asked me to—but I still don't understand why—"

"You're with him, aren't you?!" She shouted, interrupting me.

"What?"

"I can sense him! He's here with us!" She shouted as an arm void of any light reached from below grabbing her right leg.

"What is that?!" Lina shouted.

I drove my dagger towards it as it passed right through. I fell a few feet away as I heard Melanie scream for help behind me.

I looked at Melanie as she slowly got dragged into the soil.

The arm rose past her, enlarging as I noticed claws on its edge.

I dove towards her, grabbing her arm with all my might.

The pace wouldn't cease. No matter how hard I tried to pull and fight, the pace wouldn't cease.

Hermaeus grabbed her other arm as we both pulled with all our strength. The floor beneath me cracked as I placed my feet firmly in a position of power.

I couldn't help her.

Melanie looked into my eyes for one last time before she disappeared. The suns that used to shine so bright, extinguished. The light that emphasized her hope diminished.

She was gone. She had been dragged into the Underworld—by force.

Chapter 15: The Divine Light

We didn't have time to dwell over last night. We awoke early at dawn and made our way to Kavala.

It was a couple days out, but we had to make haste. We didn't know what was going on in the Underworld, just that we had to save Melanie. She was a stranger, but she risked her life to help us, and we couldn't ignore that. Sacrifice always comes with risk, but never answers.

With the Hellflame within our grasp, and Kavala only a few days away, our hopes were on the horizon ahead of us. We chased day and night hoping to catch up with it, but it was far too fast for us. Before we knew it, Kavala was a stone's throw away.

We took our first steps into town, using the Hellflame as a scarf for my head, protecting my identity.

"They're expecting you back, Ollius. Look at all these guards—we might have to wait till nightfall." Nikolina mentioned.

"We don't have the time for that. How are we supposed to find Triton like this?" I replied.

"We can go. We'll find Triton for you." Herm spoke up, volunteering him and Lina.

"That's dangerous—"

"They haven't seen our face, Ollius. Only yours."

Hesitating, I agreed. I didn't like the idea of someone risking their neck for me.

Nikolina and Herm set out not long after as me and Cilla awaited their return in a broken-down home outside the city.

Day turned to night, and night into day. Not a word from Herm or Nikolina. I was worried they were in danger, but Cilla was adamant they were not.

"We should go help them Ci. What if they were caught?"

"Don't you think something would've changed within the city if they were?"

She was right—but I couldn't shake the feeling of danger. What if Triton was no longer in this city? What if Herm was seen the night he led me around the city?

"I've heard so many stories about this place." Cilla spoke up, hoping to distract me as she looked outside towards Kavala.

"Stories?"

"Well, more like myths really. Kavala was once the most prominent city to stand within Baylor." She continued.

"What happened?"

She chuckled, "A politician was hung up to a tree with his wrists slit open."

"Surely that wasn't enough to demerit the town?"

"No. It wasn't, but that was just the beginning."

"Of what?"

"Nobody knows, really. Everyone has their own idea, or speculations. Some claim to have seen it—but nobody knows. They call it the Horn."

"The Horn? That's an interesting name."

"Before every death, every man, woman, and child in the city heard a horn sound through the streets. Every single citizen would freeze as the wrath of the Gods would take another victim. They'd pray on their knees hoping to see the next sunrise."

"This actually happened? When did it stop?"

"I never said it did. Till this day, the Horn sounds."

"That can't be. Otherwise, the Kavalians would've left long ago."

"It's not that simple. Every family here is cursed to stay. If they were to leave—they are to bear witness to a horrible tragedy befalling their family."

"Creepy."

"Indeed. But they're just stories. Apparently, talking about it is enough to actually summon the Horn—but I've never found that to be the case."

Those were the last words Cilla spoke to me before she fell asleep by my side, resting her head on my shoulder.

I finally found the courage to close my eyes and allow sleep to overtake me.

Sometime throughout the night, I awoke to distant sound of horns blaring through the city. It sounded as if death was marching through the streets. I heard children cry in unison and the sounds of battle rage.

Cilla was already awake, her dagger to her side.

"What's going on?"

"It's the Horn. Grab your blade, we need to be ready."

I grabbed the small dagger I kept in my boot and rose it to my side as I stood behind the door, crouched down.

"Do you think it's after us? We're not within the city." I whispered.

"I don't think it cares where we are, Ollius. Be prepared."

I stood there, motionless for a good amount of time, worried of making the wrong move and putting Cilla at risk.

"What if it's after Herm and Lina? We should go help them!"

"We don't know what it's after. No use in putting ourselves at risk."

"I won't stand idle for much longer, Cilla. My comrades might need me!"

"You're not leaving. Get that through your thick skull. There's a lot at risk here."

"Yeah. Our comrades—"

"No. You!" She interrupted.

"What?"

"You are the missing piece—it was never the Gem."

"Then why keep me on the sidelines? What's the point of my strength if I can't use it to fight?"

"Sparta only lost to the League because we refused to use our strongest weapon. We won't make that mistake again by allowing you to get yourself killed."

"Get myself killed? Do you even know what I am?!" I shouted as I broke through the door, sending it off its hinges.

"You're not a God Ollius! I don't care what Gaia told you!"

"What?"

"I know what she told you. I heard it myself."

"You were there?"

"That's not important! I can't let you risk the Legion for your own selfish desires!" She shouted at me.

"Who are we if not our desire, Ci? We live, bleed, die by our desire. I will not let my comrades fight on their own when there is a chance I can save them!"

"Then I'm coming with you. I need to make sure you don't get yourself killed."

"As if anything could kill me—" I uttered those words as beams of fire erupted behind me, sending me forwards towards Cilla.

I could feel an aching pain in my leg—actual pain, something I had yet to experience since my fight with Nikolaus.

"You're not going anywhere." A voice spoke through the chaos as I felt weak and exhausted. My eyes, blurry—I could see an outline of a man walking towards me. The voice was cold, empty of any emotion. What power could they wield as to incapacitate me like so?

"Ollius!" I heard Cilla shout as the flames roared.

"Ci, you need to go!" I shouted back as I stretched my right arm towards her.

"That's not happening!" I heard as through my limited vision I saw Cilla jump towards the mysterious man before he impulsively grabbed her by the neck, slamming her into the ground below.

I heard a crack.

I heard a crack.

Before I could react, my arms went numb, my body collapsed. I couldn't muster up any strength. I needed to see if Cilla was okay, but I couldn't find the strength to move. My Crimson Rage was nowhere to be found. I laid my arms to my side, weak and helpless.

I looked up as I saw the man approach, squatting in front of me. I could only see his smile through the shadows.

As he approached closer, I caught a glimpse of his eyes.

A divine white. A divine white so familiar it shot goosebumps through my back. The pain disappeared; I was starstruck by what I was seeing. Chaos stood in those white irises. A mystical presence, thriving for disarray.

The contradiction of the deceiving light still raging even after eighteen years had passed.

That's when I heard the horns blaring through my ears, signaling the reaper's arrival.

Signaling the death of Cilla of the Helm.

Those green eyes were stripped from the world, leaving behind two lifeless orbs, never again enjoying light.

He took Cilla from the world.

The horns only got louder as the realization set in.

He took Cilla from me.

I failed Nikolaus—and in those final moments as I was looking into his eyes, I promised to never allow it to happen again, and yet, here I lay mere feet away from the corpse of another comrade.

It happened again.

My eyes lit up, fighting against the hold he had against me. I felt the world turn against me at that moment. I felt reality itself disagree with the idea of someone like me existing. Time and time again I got the wrong side of the coin, and I grew tired of flipping it.

This was not a battle of strength; it was a battle of wills.

I had far too many final stands. I'd been pushed to the edge time and time again, and I was sick of balancing over the cliff.

"Give up—your body is useless now. The strength you're fighting so hard for will only be stripped away from you."

"You coward. You coward!" I shouted as I slammed my fist into the ground with the little strength I had.

The man broke into a maniacal laughter before continuing,

"A coward? You call me a coward? Is this no different from slaying a barn animal? Do you mortals even understand your contradictions?"

"'Mortals.' You're a God, aren't you?" I spoke through sips of pain.

"A God? You think I'm a God? No, boy. I don't wait for the clouds to part. I don't pretend to care; I make it known that I don't. The Gods deserted you long ago. They sit in their thrones, soaking in the blood, sweat, and tears you sacrifice for them, all while feeding you the same struggles you pray against. If you ask me, that's a far greater evil than any blood I've drawn. A false hope, a false pariah—that's what they sell you."

I stood to my knees, finding strength in every moment.

"Your name. I need your name."

"My name is nothing to you, boy." The voice spoke back, deeper now, resonating inside my head.

"Give me your name." I demanded as I finally stood to my knees.

"I don't have a name anymore, I used to go by Arrack, but that was a long time ago."

A silence preluded,

"Arrack. You're not seeing daylight."

The man laughed, falling to his knees as he held his stomach.

I stared at him, my eyes only darkening. My crimson light mixing into the whites of his.

The man stood back up, wiping his eyes and walking towards me, raising a blade I could not spot through the moonlight. As he swung his blade, it struck me—but not me.

One of my soldiers took the blow, as the other clone of me stuck a dagger through his back.

"I told you, you're not seeing daylight."

Arrack spat out blood as he landed in front of me, the white disappearing from his eyes.

I took his light, as he took hers.

I ran to Cilla, falling to my knees next to her, raising her head to mine.

"Ci, talk to me. You're fine—you have to be." I said as I held her, my eyes tearful. My arms outstretched around her body, gripping her close.

Somewhere along the way, after leaving my cage—I got lost. This is not who I was supposed to be. I was destined for more, I was destined to be Ollius, the Gallant. I was destined to bring back Sparta—that was my destiny.

Dimitris told me I was supposed to be the hero. I was supposed to be their savior. That was the expectation given to me when I took on his son's name.

That is the story I chose—forgetting no one ever gets to write their own. Looking up at the stars above me, I was reminded that those stories weren't written by heroes. They were written by the bystanders, the saved. They have no idea what the hero lost that day, only what they gave.

To be a hero, is to sacrifice everything you have, everything you would be—for the sake of others. You are expected to give up everything, otherwise you're labeled a coward—a false prophet, a martyr, a letdown.

I felt as if I lost another piece of myself at that moment.

There was a quiet silence. It's difficult to explain. I felt my emotions take control. The aching pain inside my heart exploded as my eyes lost their light. Tears strolled down my face, leaving me an empty mess. I felt the tension in my fingertips expel, the sharp dagger in my arm dropping—the distinct clink of the steel bouncing off Cilla's *Uprising,* clashing for the final time.

She was gone.

My heart broke. I can still remember the moment it all changed. The moment my heart was torn in two.

I remember the wind blowing through my dark black hair. I remember the grip I had on her arm slipping as her head hit the grass below. I remember the promises I made to her. I remember the crown that I promised her—the life I promised her.

I would never forgive myself.

I lost control. I don't remember much after seeing the light from Ci's eyes had disappeared. I saw red, and my body was no longer mine to control. Whatever anger I was holding back—whatever throbbing agony I felt inside my chest was released. I awoke to flames all around me. A throbbing ember mere feet away joining alongside the chaos surrounding it. In my peripheral I saw a scorched body, with screams in the near distance.

I became the Horn.

The heat of the fire around me made it difficult to breathe, I coughed sending my eyes to the body in my lap, a dagger struck through its chest. *My* dagger.

It was an unfamiliar face, but I was sure it was innocent. I did it again, *I hurt more innocent people.* More blood stained my hands that night.

I couldn't control the anger inside me, because even in this moment it swelled. A burning fury—a resilience to peace. I didn't know how to feel. I felt the monster inside my scream, as the voice inside my head only begged for it to stop. I dropped the body, crawling back—I grabbed my head screaming into the night sky. Houses burned all around me, crumbling to the ground.

Kavala was no more.

Cilla was no more.

The Son of Sparta was a traitor of fortune, a merchant of massacre and a reaper for Death himself.

I stood up; my knees weak from exhaustion. I took steps through the town—torn and destroyed into pieces. Blood and other atrocities stained the rock walls of the alleys I walked through searching for Herm and Lina.

Cilla was gone, I couldn't get that thought out of my head. I kept reliving it, repeatedly. My head felt loud as the sound of her back breaking repeated inside my skull. I was on the verge of tears as I found myself collapsing, unable to think clearly. So many of my thoughts raced at once, it was overwhelming.

She was gone. There was nothing I could ever do to bring her back, and that realization hurt more than losing her.

I felt actual pain inside my chest—emotional agony that I couldn't soothe. I dove my arms in a nearby bucket hoping to wash off the stained blood on my hands—yet Cilla's wouldn't leave. Why wouldn't her blood wash off my hands?

I couldn't breathe. My eyes got blurry, as I felt my chest tighten. What was this feeling? What was going on? I blanked in and out of consciousness trying to take hold of myself once again.

I shot up running through the town as fast as I could shouting for Herm.

Flames erupted in front of me, forcing the house to my side to collapse. Loud sounds of wood split as a man of thirty fell towards me, landing in my arms.

I put him down, as respectful as I can be to his deceased corpse.

I pulled the debris away, crawling through a tiny hole I managed to create. I kept running through the streets, hoping none of the bodies I passed were my friends.

I eventually heard voices shout through the chaos of an entire city burning.

I vaulted over a stall, turning the corner to crash into Herm, colliding into each other.

"Ollius. What happened?!"

"I don't know. I think I caused all of this."

"What do you mean?" He asked as I saw the fires in the background reflect off his brown eyes.

"I don't remember anything. I saw Cilla—" I couldn't get the words out, "I lost control." I said, stuttering.

"Cilla? What do you mean?"

My head got loud again, a siren blaring inside my skull—I grabbed it in pain.

"Ollius. Get up—let's get you out of here."

"No! I failed her, Herm!" I shouted as I felt a tear crawl down my face. My eyes lit up, although— not the same color as usual.

"Your eyes. It was dark, I couldn't tell—you're not Ollius—who are you?!" Herm asked as he stepped away, reaching for his blade.

"What are you talking about?" I replied, standing up.

"Stay back!"

"What's wrong?"

"Your eyes—they're different!"

I reached my arm up towards it, as the light that bounced off my skin was not the same crimson one I knew.

I ran to the water well next to me, looking into it, I saw the same deceiving light of the man I slew. A divine white yet contradicted with the strongest sense of evil I could imagine. A familiar evil, one I stood face to face with only a couple months ago.

I turned around towards Herm—his face worried and determined. Determined to bring his friend back, reaching towards the darkest trenches in the slightest hope I can be saved.

"You need to leave, Herm. You're in danger."

"No. I won't leave your side, Ollius. I'll save you."

"You can't save me Herm. It's too late for me. Arracks got his claws dug deep. I can win, I know I can—but I won't be able to stop myself from hurting you."

"That's not who we are, Ollius. You said it yourself; if we keep the same mindset of leaving behind our brothers in arms, we'll never win. I trust you more than anyone else in my life, I know what you're capable of, and that won't scare me. I'm here."

There was a silence before I continued, "Herm. This isn't the time for that. I can't lose anyone else, if I hurt you, I'll never recover."

"Then don't."

"It's not that simple—!"

"It never is, Ollius!" Herm interrupted,

"But it's all you've ever done. You're stronger than this monster inside you. You used to never believe anything could stop you, you used to believe that nothing could control you—that you were a God amongst men!"

"I'm unstoppable, Herm—that's the problem!"

"No, it's not. You only lost control when you thought you lost Cilla."

"I didn't think I lost her, Herm. I saw her die. I saw the light leave her eyes—she's gone, and it's my fault."

"She's been with us since the beginning, you idiot! She left with us!"

The world around me stopped. Halted, by euphoria I never thought possible. A relief soared through my spine lifting a strain off my back—an exhale of grief and sorrow. The clouds parted, revealing the moonlight as it spotlighted a bright red rose mere feet in front of me. In front of my eyes, I saw it wither away. Its crimson petals disintegrated as the lively stem crumbled into dust.

I looked up into Hermaeus' eyes as I felt the deceiving light erupt into an imperishable rage. Another stalemate in the battle of wills. My will to live amongst my brethren, and Arracks will to spread terror through the land.

The battle waged as I fell back grabbing and holding onto the well behind me in hopes of maintaining my balance.

Eventually, I felt the divine light leave my sight, my crimson light returning yet again.

I was out of breath as Hermaeus reached me—having fought my toughest battle to date—and yet no blood shed other than the innocents I slayed under the control of Arrack.

As we walked through the town, the fire now almost all extinguished, I couldn't help but wonder where Arrack had disappeared to. According to Herm, Cilla had originally left with them and was now helping Triton save some of the villagers trapped all around the town. The entire night was a ruse by Arrack to eventually force me to do his bidding. He was hoping to leave me as an empty shell of a man, making it easier to manipulate day by day as I wallowed in my sorrow.

If it wasn't for Herm, I don't think I could've made it out. I was so angry; I was filled with so much agony I couldn't find a way to think comprehensively. Thinking back to earlier, I had so many thoughts crowding my head, I couldn't focus on walking.

I never realized how much Cilla meant to me—how much they all meant to me. After Nikolaus, I lost a comrade, a brother in arms, a warrior of fine strength for my Legion, I was worried I'd lose my home, my friends—I just never realized I was worried about losing myself, but did I even know who that was?

I knew my name, and the goal that kept me fighting every day, but I didn't know who Ollius was. Since I left the cage, I never got the chance to even try to understand who I am. I don't know myself—as weird as that sounds, I don't know Ollius. I never tried to.

I'm a best friend to Herm, I'm a warrior for the Legion, an avenger for Sparta—but those are all what I am to other people, not who I am for myself.

I think that's why I lost it. Sure, losing Cilla hurt, but it wasn't the only factor. In that moment, I lost a piece of who I am—a piece of who I think I am—and that thought scared me.

At the end of the day, I only really care about myself. As selfish as that is, it's who I am, and I understand that now. I am a selfish person, but I'm okay with that. If it's who I am, who I was created and destined to be then I accept it. With all my faults, I accept myself.

That was the start of understanding who I really am. It's not humility, it's acceptance. It's not an ego, it's confidence. I let Arrack get inside my head, and it took Herm risking his own life to realize I got inside my own. I should've never lost faith in who I am.

Chapter 16: The Skip

The massacre of the Kavalians was done by my hand. The entire city was burnt to a crisp in a fit of rage I had no control over. The words of Gaia came back to me in a whirlwind of warning,

"With power always comes sacrifice."

Never did her words make more sense, for I realized alongside my strength came a cost. To some, that cost would be a reasonable sum, to someone like me, it's a steep price. The more life I take, the more control I lose. I can feel it creeping at this very moment. Right beneath my spine lies a monster. A monster of undeniable strength, and an increasing appetite for chaos, for war. This monster doesn't have a name, it doesn't breathe, or fight, or even move. It merely exists to spread agony through my rage. I had no answer, or solution for it. I could only push it deeper into my subconscious. I could only ignore it as my fury invited it to the surface.

It was my Olympian blood.

My power was not normal. It was not magic—it could not be replicated by any sorcerer known to man.

My power, as Gaia had mentioned, can only be created by an Olympian.

I wasn't sure who I was to Olympus. Melanie told me I had a place to take after my time in Baylor was done. The Sage told me my race would come to an end—but I cared little for prophecies.

I don't know what I'm destined for, nobody does. A life's not worth living if you know the ending. Once you realize your future—your present becomes fixated on changing it. You could die surrounded by every child you created, and grandchildren that followed, by your wealth, and your kingdom—and none of it will matter in that final moment. Nobody gets a happy ending, there are always regrets. In that final breath—the final inhale you summon all the unrealized potential you failed to bring to life. In that final inhale, you conjure up all the regrets you can never succeed. In the final inhale, your eyes grow cold as you see there are dreams you never had the chance to accomplish. In that final inhale, you breathe in all your mistakes.

Then the day comes that your grandchild lies on his deathbed to remember you for the final time before he takes his final inhale—your memory becoming lost to history. Everything you ever did, changed, fixed won't matter. Your name will become a staple in a haystack of other mediocre people who worked mediocre jobs and lived mediocre lives.

That is the truth of life—you are born to die. You fulfill your ambitions so you may live on through a legacy no one will care about as much as you.

We made it out of Kavala as fast as we could, heading towards the coast so we may strike down the Kraken with Triton. We found a nearby ship that we took over. Its' previous occupants a victim of my massacre.

We needed its eye, and Triton needed his sword back.

Seeing Tri for the first time since we escaped prison, I had no words for him. My brain was scrambled with the lives I just took. The number of bodies I had to crawl through to find my Circle was a number I did not want to count.

I felt an immeasurable amount of guilt. It wasn't my choice, but it was still my arm that drove so many to beg for mercy. I burned their homes—I took their lives. That was my sin to bear.

"So, the Kraken?" Cilla spoke up next to me as I stared out into the sea.

"Yeah. I tried defeating him myself, but I ended up losing my blade before I got the chance to see him."

"How did you lose your blade?" Cilla asked.

"I dropped it."

"Where?"

"In the sea."

"Okay." Cilla said, ending the conversation.

"Why were you trying to fight it to begin with? You realize it's a mythical creature, right? No one even knows if it even really exists." Herm asked as he crossed his arms.

"I can't really say. I don't know you that well yet."

"We're helping you defeat the Kraken. You owe us that much." Cilla spoke up.

"I don't owe you guys anything. *You* owe me."

Cilla scoffed,

"I don't trust you—"

"I never asked you to." Triton interrupted.

"Calm down. We've got work to do. How do we find this Kraken?" I asked still looking towards the sea.

"We don't. It finds us." Tri answered.

"You're kidding." Lina replied.

"Nope. There's no way to summon the Kraken. It's a mythical creature—little is known about it."

"We can't sit around all day, Tri."

"It's the only choice we have."

"That's not going to cut it. I need more."

"More?"

"That's what I said, yes, I need more."

"Who do you think you're speaking to, Ollius?"

"You don't want the answer to that."

"Don't forget, that was my town you butchered, Ollius."

I chuckled as I turned around towards him.

"You're threatening me?"

"I wouldn't call it a threat. More of a promise, really." Triton said as he took a step towards me.

I conquered the space between us as I looked into his ocean blue eyes,

"And what would that be?"

"After we kill the Kraken, I am going to drive my blade inside your skull, Ollius of Sparta."

"Many have tried, Triton. None have survived."

"None were as capable as me. I don't care if you weren't in control, those were still my brothers that were killed in cold blood!"

"Do you wish to join them then?" I asked as I raised my eyebrow. I was ready to add his head to my collection at a moment's notice. I would not be disrespected.

"Enough!" Herm shouted as he came between us.

"This isn't getting anywhere! Stop it!" Lina shouted.

I chuckled as I walked away towards the deck.

Triton scoffed as he walked towards the wheel.

Lina looked towards Cilla, puzzled and frustrated.

"What?" Cilla asked.

"Why didn't you try to stop them?"

Cilla didn't give Lina a response and merely sat next to me on the edge of the boat.

We sat in silence for the longest time, waiting for anything to happen.

"I would do the same, you know." She said as she peeked towards me.

"What?"

"Come on. You really thought Herm could keep something like that a secret?"

"It's not what you think."

"Yet it is."

I didn't know what to say. I kept silent.

"There are only two constants in this world, Ollius. Death, and dishonesty. I accept that. I understand we all lie to benefit or escape—but we shouldn't lie to ourselves. It wasn't you, don't deceive yourself."

"What do you mean?"

"You don't care about the lives you took. That's the last thing on your mind. You're angry that you could lose control to anything—to be fooled into doing someone's dirty work."

I again sat quiet. I had no words.

"You're not a good person; nobody said you had to be. That's not who we are, as Spartans. Our people conquered, murdered, drove nations to their knees. Why do you think they created the Achaean League? That's who we're trying to revive. Historians and story tellers called us the Devil's Advocate. The bringers of chaos and destruction—given the power of the Gods, we were a danger to the mortal realm. If I was in their shoes, I would've done the same thing. Yet I fight everyday—contradicting myself."

"You've never talked this much before." I said, looking down.

"Maybe I've finally got something to say."

I sat in quiet yet again, feeling the daggers of Tritons eyes dig their treacherous fingers into the side of my head. I couldn't believe I'd have to kill him, but I wouldn't lie down to be kicked any longer.

The bright day turned to gray in an instant. Clouds drove into the sky in a terrifying pace. The calm waters from before rose as if commanded by the God of the Sea. Ahead of us was a gigantic humanoid figure built up of sea water mere feet from our small ship. He held a trident in his right arm, and Triton's blade in his left.

"It's him, prepare yourselves!" Herm shouted as he reached for his blade.

"Give me your blade, Herm."

"What? No."

"Give me your blade, now." I demanded as I extended my palm towards him.

"Fine." Herm said as he gave it up, pouting.

I felt a connection to Herm's blade. It felt right, pure, maybe even safe.

I walked towards the beast as it rose its Trident in the air, summoning a gust of air followed by a lightning bolt, enchanting the strength of its mighty fork.

It launched the bolt towards me as it met Herm's blade, enveloping the electricity.

I drove the sword through the figure as it collapsed into a puddle of water onto the deck. Triton's blade landing next to my foot.

"Some mythical creature." I said as I chuckled and kicked the blade towards Tri.

Tri caught the blade in his left arm, pointing it towards the sky.

"That's just the beginning, Son of Sparta."

In unison, we all looked above us.

In the sky, there was a faint oval. A small distinction, slowly growing.

"No." Herm muttered under his breath.

"It can't be."

"I told you I never got the chance to see it, because it destroyed my boat before it could even open its eye."

The wind soared all around us, as lightning struck in every direction.

I could hear the wood of the ship chipping as the wind only got faster.

"We need to get out of here Tri!" Herm shouted through the obnoxious sound of wind tearing through our eardrums.

"We can't. We've committed!"

"You don't understand! Linas here! She's not a fighter!" Hermaeus grabbed Tri by the shirt.

"That's not my problem." Tri said as he pushed Herm away in one swift movement.

"How do we beat it?" I asked as I stared into, quite literally, the eye of the storm.

"I don't know. Our best bet is to wait for its eye to open and strike then."

"It's so high up, how do we hurt it?"

"Let me worry about that. Just prepare to fight."

"What am I preparing for?"

"Things you've never seen before."

I smirked as I walked towards Herm, returning his blade.

He nodded towards me as he took off with his beloved.

I looked towards the creature as I felt an inkling of silver touch my hand.

I looked to my right palm as I saw Triton sliding a blade into my hands.

"I don't need this anymore. It'll make Hammy jealous."

I nodded, before I felt the sea rise around me, shaking the boat we had climbed on.

"Don't worry, we'll stay afloat."

There was a shield of water all around us, shielding us from the rageful waves created by the Kraken, but also creating a gateway for the creatures of the sea to attack.

I looked forward as a crab dived towards me.

I struck it down with my blade as more and more creatures piled onto our boat, surrounding us.

There were gigantic crabs that stood easily two feet tall, with a blue embellish to their shell. Alongside stood turquoise humanoid figures with fins for feet and gills stuck to the side of their neck, sharks poking their head out of the shield, foxes with blue fur that sat atop, glaring their deceiving eyes towards us.

Every single one of the brutes had a white divine light, with a tint of ocean blue in their eyes.

"They're Whispers of Poseidon! Strike their eyes, it's their only weak spot." Triton announced as his blade transformed into a hammer.

I looked forward as another Whisper dived towards me, another crab. I drove my blade through it, entirely.

I used my boot to slide it off my silver blade, as I elbowed another. We were being overtaken by Whispers.

For the next few minutes, we slashed away, filling the entire deck with the lifeless corpses of Whispers.

A shark dove towards Cilla before I grabbed its jaw, ripping it into two, turning into a puddle.

We stood back-to-back-to-back. The three of us fighting alongside one another as the Whispers kept coming.

"How long till they stop?!" I shouted.

"I don't know, I've never gotten this far! Just keep fighting!" Triton ordered as he slammed his hammer into a Whisper, crushing it, leaving a splash of water as its remains.

Eventually, the Whispers slowed down, and I heard a terrifying screech atop me.

The Kraken was opening its eye.

A gorgeous gray color looked down towards us. Almost as if enveloped by a sorrow we couldn't understand. A sphere of gray inside an orb of divine white. An ashy gray, as if coral long deceased, thousands of feet into the sky, it acknowledged us as a worthy opponent.

"We need that eye."

"Where would you keep it?" Triton said, laughing.

"Shut up."

"I've got something. Problem is, I only have one shot at it." Triton announced as he reached for his back pocket.

"Then make it count. This moment decides everything."

Inside my chest I felt danger close in. My heart rang fast as I looked around to realize the warning. Left, right, I couldn't find it, and yet my heart beat senselessly.

"Somethings coming!"

In an instant, I looked above towards the eye as through the storm brewing around it an arm built of clouds broke through.

The Kraken was materializing—getting stronger every moment. His eye glared at us as rain splattered into the ocean around us.

"How are we supposed to defeat this thing?" Cilla asked, hopelessly.

"I don't know—I just know we have to. I don't care how strong it is, we have to believe we're stronger." I answered as I clenched the blade in my palm.

I looked to Tri as he squatted over a puddle mumbling words under his tongue.

"What're you doing?"

Tri ignored me, continuing his abnormal ritual. He pulled a brown bag out from his back pocket, unraveling it. Inside was a white powder, one I can smell from where I stood, a distinct scent I immediately caught on to, it was sulfur. Tri poured it into the puddle as a weapon began materializing.

"Forgive me, Hammy. This calls for a different approach."

From the puddle rose a trident, embellished with gold and diamonds, tinted by a turquoise aura.

"What is that?" I asked as I walked towards him.

"Ten minutes, Ollius. It's all I've got with this. If the Kraken is not slayed by then, we lose."

I rose my blade to the eye,

"Then what are we waiting for?"

I heard Tri smirk as he rose the trident to the sky, water rising alongside it around our ship.

Suddenly, I heard booms from all around the ship, sending the ocean into a spiral of rage. Poseidon's fury was on display for all to see!

"What's happening?"

I ran to the side of the ship as I saw we were rising.

It was phenomenal, Triton was lifting a cube of water. It was a holy sight, and it sent shivers down to my knees. There was a singular cube rising, sucking up all the water in the surrounding area.

Triton was quite literally turning the sea on its side.

"What are you?" Cilla asked, starstruck.

"Dangerous." He laughed maniacally as we rose to meet the Kraken.

The Kraken sent its fist towards us as Tri jumped to meet it, the collision between the cloudy arm of the Kraken and the trident sent both flying back.

I caught Tri before he could fall off the ship.

"What is that thing?"

"*The Bernadette*, it's said this once belonged to Poseidon himself. Before his son stole it, of course."

"Are you kidding? You're telling me your—"

"I haven't told you anything." Tri interrupted.

I let him go,

"So, what's the plan? We stab him in the eye?" I asked as Tri walked towards the deck.

"No. I stab it in the eye." He said, followed by a silence. I could tell defeating the Kraken meant more to him than my revenge meant to me. He was a man of purpose with a mission he needed to complete against all odds. There was intention in those ocean blue eyes.

"Alright. Tell me what you need."

"Be ready to catch me. Cilla, take the wheel. Where you command, the ocean will follow. Ollius, take care of Hammy. He gets lonely."

"Wait what?"

Tri threw me the Hammerhead as he dove off the ship to be picked up by a stream of water that enveloped him, with the *Bernadette* as the spear, sending him at an unfathomable speed towards the eye.

The Kraken tried to react and close his lid, but it was too late. The *Bernadette* was the heart of the sea, it couldn't be overpowered, especially in its domain. A burst of blue light drove the skies to a fearful retreat.

That's the last I remember before I awoke to calm seas. From my side I could hear scraping, and water splashing to the side of the ship I laid onto.

"He's up!" I heard a feminine voice shout from above me.

My eyes weak, the world shot back into view as I saw Cilla's beautiful green eyes stare back into mine.

"Cilla?" I asked as I reached towards her face.

"You're fine, stand up." She chuckled as she stood up, my head dropping from her lap to hit the rock-hard wood below.

I grabbed my head in pain as I sat up to see an empty sea, rid of any Kraken or Whisper.

I turned around to see Cilla stand above me, and Triton at the edge of the boat, holding his Hammerhead blade, sharpening it with a white cluster of rock.

To his side was Hermaeus with his arm over the shoulder of Lina.

We were docked, our boat leeching onto the coast.

"What happened?"

"Triton defeated the Kraken and when I looked back down you were knocked out. I don't actually know why—"

"The eye! Did we get it?" I interrupted as I stood up hastily.

Triton threw me the white cluster of rock he was holding. Touching it I was electrified. It hurt and I dropped it as I felt my fingertips burn as if stuck into a bowl of fire.

"What's wrong?" Cilla asked as she closed in.

"I don't know. It burned my fingertips."

"The Eye?"

"That's the Eye?" I asked as I held my fingers.

"Yeah. I had to dig deep to find that one." Tri responded.

"Then we have everything we need." I said as a blanket of silence overtook the atmosphere. A realization entered our ambience, we were finally capable of entering the Underworld.

"Are we actually doing this?" Nikolina asked as she stood up, crossing her arms, invoking a defensive stance.

"What choice do we have?" I replied as I pushed onto my knee, standing up.

"We can stop here!" Herm blurted.

"We can't afford to. You know that." I turned towards him.

"Then it's really time." Herm exhaled, fearful of what's to come.

"I can go alone. There's no reason for all of us to get trapped in the underworld." I reasoned.

"You know we can't let that happen." Cilla argued.

"This is your last chance to turn back. After this, there's a chance we're trapped there for eternity."

The group went silent.

"We've come this far, Ollius. I'm not turning back, but I think Ci and Lina should."

"How dare you?" Lina shouted, as she turned her head towards him.

"I feel as if I lost a piece of myself that night, as if I lost hope that night. My twin brother was taken from me, his life stripped in front of my very eyes. I don't have much to fight for anymore, other than to extinguish the pain inside my heart. I don't want to stand idly by and let someone else do what I'm supposed to do. He was your friend, Herm, but he was my brother!"

"Just calm down, that's not what I was insinuating—"

"I don't care what you were insinuating! I'm sorry if I gave you the impression that I do!"

Herm stood, a little shocked.

"Enough. This isn't going anywhere." I interrupted.

"We're all going to the Underworld."

Chapter 17: Damnation

It was simple. We had the Hell flame, and the Eye of the Kraken. All we needed now was to find out a way to contact Hades by using these two.

Herm had the idea of going back up to see the Sage, but after our last conversation, and the fact that the entire cabin disappeared, I didn't hold out hope that he'd be there to answer.

We were at a dead-end. We didn't know what our next step was. Triton took off, an uneasy smile residing on his face. He felt satisfied with the Krakens' slaughter, and none of us knew why.

It was decided after Lina presented it, that the best course of action was to bring back the two items to Matullus and hope for the best. He was highly praised by the members of my Circle, and I had yet to find out why for there were many formidable characters back at camp, although sorcerers were few and far between.

So, we took to the road once again. After all the walking I've done since I left my cage, I was getting a little sick of it. It seemed as soon as I left my confinement, I embarked on one long journey on an excruciatingly long road. I've gotten used to the sounds of dirt crunching beneath my feet, to the point where I've found a beauty in it. Every step I took only brought me closer to Hades—I could feel it, it was as if I could feel him taunting me even now. Hades was within my soul, hopefully getting tormented by the eternal flames he'd lit with his own hands.

We made our way back to the camp after days of walking in silence. Every step we took we envisioned the horrors we'd have to witness in the coming days. The same crunch we found love within only reminded us of the bones the Dragon crunched on during his massacre.

Since the beginning, so much blood has been shed. From the glory days of Sparta, to the collapse, to the revival. On both sides, the pool of blood only grew thicker.

The Will of Sparta had been born rageful and was now only eager to die. So much battle, and so much strength lost in its eternal chase for power and control. Sparta was not on the right side of history, so that made us, the Legion, devils in the history books. We were looking to bring back that rage—to light the flame long extinguished in the horrors of war. What a thing that irony is—for the exact thing Sparta sought was what drove it out of existence. That pain King Ag spread through the lands was a thing of unnatural compulsion.

We made it back, knocking on the large wooden doors of the Legion, we only felt empty. We wanted Matullus to know nothing of how to reach the Underworld—for it meant we get to live alongside our compatriots another day, but to do so was to turn back on the hopes of Sparta.

We were quiet when we arrived, heading straight to Matullus. His residence was that of a tent, mere feet from the Town Hall. Inside, he spent day in and day out studying sorcery.

Walking inside, the tent was empty. We found books scattered across the floors, and old food in the cabinets.

"I can't help you." We heard from behind us.

"You must. We don't have any other options here." Lina pleaded.

"There's no way out. If I get you in—you can't leave."

"I know. We are very aware of it." I chimed in, turning my head towards him.

Matullus stood at a breezy 5'10. He was lean and had a very particular beard. I couldn't understand it, but he carried an appealing charm in every step he took.

"This is what you want?" He asked as he shot his void like eyes towards me.

"No. This is what I need."

"Then I'll help, but don't say I didn't warn you."

Matullus grabbed a silk pouch from his table and ushered us to follow him.

We walked outside where the entire Legion had their eyes stuck to us. Thomas stood, on crutches watching us with almost tearful eyes.

"Matullus told us you were on your way back. He was up all night trying to find you a way to the Underworld." Thomas explained.

"We're ready."

"You sure you don't want to rest first? This could be the last time we'll see you." Matullus said as he bent down to the ground pouring sulfur from the pouch.

I looked to my companions, determined and motivated eyes met mine.

"We're ready." I repeated.

Isaiah, the kid from before, walked over to me, handing me a backpack after telling me it was full of food and other necessities we'd need down there.

"I can only get you a conference with him, the rest is up to you. Just remember, you get one shot at this Ollius." Matullus said as he grabbed the Hellflame from me, and the Eye from Herm.

"I only need one."

Some time went by as Matullus worked on the spell. It smelled so bad I almost threw up. I looked all around me to see concerned faces. The Legion didn't want us to go. They wanted us to stay safe, just like we had kept them for so long. These men and women were my people. They were the last Remnants of Sparta, and I didn't care what kind they were. They accepted me, they gave me a home, a reason—a purpose—a fight. As far as I was concerned, my life was theirs. My life belonged to them—and whether I risk it was not a choice, it was a given.

"Okay. It's done."

"Well, where is he?"

"Take the eye and drive it with all your might into the robe when you're ready." Matullus instructed as he took a step away.

I looked around for one last time, receiving a nod from Herm.

I grabbed the Eye, almost tearing my arm into two as I sent it towards the Hellflame, fire erupting as if the cosmos were introduced to life for the first time.

I felt the ground shake below me as some homes collapsed upon themselves in the near distance. Wind sheered past us, blowing Matullus' robe up, revealing a scimitar in his sheathe.

The chaos halted at a moment's notice.

There was a silence as the clouds combined—turning day into night.

The Eye was gone, the Hellflame alongside it, leaving only ashes burning brighter every second.

The flame from the ashes grew as I could see a humanoid figure through the fire—although minimal.

It was quiet as the entire Legion looked upon us.

"You brought it back to me, I am eternally grateful to you, Son of Sparta." A voice spoke, beaming of bass and menace. The voice was heavy, the dawn of millions of tortured spirits in its wake.

"You disgust me with every word you speak, Hades."

"That's not the proper way to speak to a God. You should know better."

"Let me in." I commanded as I took a step towards the flame.

"You want passage through my realm?"

"No. I want passage *to* your realm."

Hades chuckled, "Brave."

"My rage is everlasting Hades, and everything you've done—you will suffer for. You *will* beg."

"So many have tried, all have failed. Including your father—"

"Don't you dare mention my father if you're not willing to speak his name!" I interrupted shouting into the flames.

"Raise your voice again, and the Legion will feel my wrath."

"As if—"

"I wasn't finished!" Hades thundered, "You escaped the cage I built for you, just to spend the entire time working for someone else. You wasted your chance at freedom, so why are you so eager to walk into another cage? Maybe you can't help but be a pawn."

"You caged me?"

"You really don't know? I almost feel bad for you." Hades said, following with maniacal laughter. "Do you even know what you are? Your pal, Demetris—how do you think he knew your fathers name when no one else did? Did you really think he was on your side?!" Hades shouted as the flames roared.

I couldn't find the words to reply. Stutters and half syllables retreated from my vocal cords—I felt my entire world collapse. My eyes were forced open, my jaw unhinged.

"I'm going to enjoy telling you this, thoroughly. I just want to make sure I can enjoy the moment."

"Tell me what you know Hades." I demanded, as I found myself on my knees—my entire balance stripped away from me.

There was a silence as I heard Hades grin. Although the figure was transparent, I just knew he was smiling.

"You were a mistake, Ollius. You were never supposed to exist."

"What do you mean?" I interrupted,

"Interrupt me again, and we're done,

Mizeria didn't take you from your home—they saved you from it. The day you were born, you were destined to be in second place. The boy of prophecy was your elder brother, and his power far exceeded that of any warrior alive. Ollius—the real one—was capable of strength beyond comparison. He was brave and powerful, he was said to even rival the Gods, and Zeus took that as a threat. To remedy, he sent his favorite son to strike him down. Ollius was powerful, but far too timid. His power was wasted on a pacifist. Sparta fell that same day—not by Greece and not by Mizeria, but by Zeus's hand. The crimson light of

Ollius' eyes withered away alongside his body, until the King found yours. Your mother was sent off to produce more children, and your father was never found again—and trust me, the truth about him would destroy your will to fight. Commander Vassilios found you after forcing your city to rubble. He saved you from the wrath of Zeus. He took you home and vowed to keep you safe. The light from your eyes turned anything, and everything to flames. You were dangerous, so he locked you away with my help. Demetris was never your guardian, he didn't even exist. You destroyed Mizeria through a fit of anger that I orchestrated. You are my pawn, Ollius—your reality is what I see fit."

Flames erupted all around me and my Circle, as a portal invited itself to the surface.

"So come on in. I am eager to meet you in person."

I fell to my knees, finally finding out the truth of my existence. Since the beginning—since the day I was born I had been a slave to Hades. I was born to fight—that's it. That's what was decided for me the day my crimson light was lit. I was a pawn—a tool.

"It can't be true. You're lying,

Demetris *was* real. He told me about the stars, he told me he'd save me!"

"No. Vassilios told you about the stars—and you tore his neck into pieces." There was a silence as I threw my arms to my head.

"That's not even the best part, in his final moments, he could only smile. All he ever wanted for you, was to find your voice. If this was it, he was more than willing to die for it."

I felt my heart drop. I couldn't breathe. My head ached, my consciousness was interrupted by a streamline of guilt. If what Hades says is true, then I was the ultimate traitor. Countless lives—so much blood has been shed by my hand. Kavala sat heavy on my head—and Mizeria never left.

I was a murderer.

I was a monster.

My head was loud, my voice overwhelming me—

Murderer. Traitor. Monster. You killed them all.
That blood will never wash off. You're tainted.

"Hades," I said fighting the ache in my head, "You will suffer a coward's death. Gather your army, build your walls—do everything in your power to stop me. It won't matter. I will use your soldiers' lifeless bodies to climb your palace. I will hold your head as I drive my silver blade into your skull. Death—that is all I can promise you. War—that is all that's left for you. Chaos—that is all I will bring you."

"Stop telling me, come show me." He replied, his voice sinking deeper.

I jumped towards the portal, forgetting everything but my blade. The portal shut, leaving my companions behind.

I was falling into a void—the sound of Hades's laughter never leaving my head. I had made my choice; I had come to fulfill my promise to Nikolaus. I was betrayed, repeatedly—without even knowing it. Anger clouded every thought that entered my membrane, leaving behind a mere promise of slaughter and chaos.

I have made my bed. All that's left is to lay in it.

Chapter 18: The Minotaur

The wind soared past my long black hair invading my ear canal. I was still in freefall, seeing nothing but a black void all around me. As I fell, I could only recall Hades words—he made me his pawn—everything around me could be fake and I'd have no idea.

What did this mean for the Legion? Were they real—or just another reality-altering delusion? It didn't matter, it didn't change anything for me. I didn't know if I believed in what Hades told me, just that he had to die.

My crimson light shined brighter than ever. I could feel myself sink deeper into the claws of rage, but I didn't care. If it meant I had the strength to take his throne, I'd gladly give myself up to my Olympian blood. I had never been this angry before—through all the blood I shed I had never felt anger like this before. I hated the way it made me feel, I felt lost for the usual freedom I chased was what kept me shackled now. This wasn't anger—it was fury. It was a battle-inducing triumph of will that could not be tied down, I would not be made a fool of, and I would not see this day to be my last.

I'm on my way Hades.

Before I could react, I landed into the ground below.

I awoke to my knees to see nothing but an empty void—where were the tormented spirits of the Underworld? The lakes of magma? The fabled flames of the Underworld?

There was absolutely nothing. I stood to my feet taking a step in an unknown direction.

It made no difference which way I walked, I was willing to crawl through every nook and cranny of this Godforsaken land if it meant finding Hades.

So I walked, my footsteps echoing into the vast unknown of this realm—every step sounding the alarms for the Merchant of Death's arrival.

It took a while before I saw any form of structure. In the near distance, I saw a stone structure that looked to resemble a sort of Colosseum. It was strangely lit, as although there was not an ounce of light or life, it was visible as if daylight struck it.

I gripped my blade tighter, anticipating the battle ahead.

As I got closer, I heard the sounds of a roaring crowd inside the Colosseum. I had an audience for the massacre I was to put forth.

Walking through the vast doorway, I noticed banners and other paraphernalia of a Minotaur strung up all around the halls and walls.

Copper. I thought as the smell of blood stained the air around me. It almost overwhelmed my senses as I only got closer to the Arena.

The Colosseum was built up of a dark stone, and a bright gray to contrast. I felt in danger as I roamed the halls. The stink of murder only got louder as I ventured deeper within. The walls were blood-stained and gory. I found a corpse pinned to a wall as I rounded a corner.

The crowd roared as I finally reached the main entrance, crossing the doorway presented to me.

Inside the Arena—there were gray skies and a crowd of hundreds surrounding an arena built up of dirt and bones.

Where did this come from? Outside the Arena, there was only a black void with no signs of life or sky. I was worried I might've made a mistake wandering into here—did I leave the Underworld?

I walked to the center as the crowd only managed to get louder cheering my name,

"Ollius! Ollius! Ollius!"

This felt eerie. Were these men and women even alive? Their skin, although healthy, had a gray tint to it, alongside their clothes.

Their eyes were built up of static and any distinguishable feature was blurred.

Before I could further analyze anything about the mysterious crowd and Colosseum, I felt a blunt pain to my left side as I flew tens of feet away landing into a pile of dirt. Dirt flew everywhere, cushioning the blow.

"Father told me you were coming. What took you so long?" A voice spoke, deep and clear.

"Father?" I said as I stood up, shaking off the aching pain in my right side. I looked up to see a creature of terrifying height.

Easily thirteen-foot tall, the behemoth stood wielding a wooden club. Horns of evergreen, and eyes of blazing suns. He carried a muscular physique, one triumphing even that of my own.

The Minotaur. I've heard stories about this creature, although none I believed to be true. Demetrius—or Vassilios—had told me tales of his ventures into the Acropolis. The murder he left in his wake was symbolic of his position as the Son of Hades. I knew Melanie had to have been lying now. For mere foot away stood her elder brother, the Minotaur of The Underworld.

He wore light armor, barely grazing the right side of his chest. His breath smelled of blood, and his unkempt hair reeked of slaughter—guts, and entrails poking out.

His grin—his uneasy, merciless grin—told stories of pain and murder. He was a true monster.

"No one's ever left the Colosseum alive. You look," He paused for a second, sizing me up before continuing, "tasty."

"Thanks," I said as I pulled my blade from a skull long decayed to my side.

The Minotaur charged toward me, his speed bulldozing me into the arena wall as the crowd booed in response. As he held me to the wall, I looked up to see a spectator wearing a gold necklace, embezzled with a turquoise gem in the middle. It was beautiful, and the only thing I could focus on was the Minotaur overpowering me.

I felt my consciousness fade as the Minotaur drove his club into my side repeatedly. I was getting beat senselessly, and I couldn't find an ounce of strength to return.

I grabbed his ankle, pulling myself between his legs in an instant.

The Minotaur turned around, his face visibly shocked.

"How did you do that?" He asked as he stumbled backwards.

"Do what?" My voice was weak and ineffective.

"You're not supposed to be able to fight back in here—how did you do that?" The Minotaur said, fear residing in his irises.

"Father made this arena specifically with me in mind, it zaps your strength, leaving you nothing but your will!" He continued, tears on the verge of his eyes.

"Why are you crying?" I said, feeling sluggish and worn out. I had no power in here, only my will kept me going. I needed to get to Hades, that's all that mattered to me, but my strength was nowhere to be found.

The Minotaur growled in response as he once again tackled and pounded me into the floor beneath my feet.

As he continued his onslaught, my eyes fell to a piece of jewelry on a skull nearby. It was a gold necklace contrasted by a turquoise gem in the center. It was familiar and carried an emphasis of sadness in its glory.

That's when I realized where I was laying.

This was not an Arena; it was a graveyard. The spectators were not bystanders, they were warriors that lost their lives in the same place I was about to lose mine.

That's why they were booing so relentlessly. I could set them free; they were relying on me.

I grabbed and crushed the Minotaur's wooden club as he swung it, I put my feet to his gut as I sent him flying over my head. My movements were slow, but I was still far stronger.

That didn't stop him from getting back up as fast as he fell.

I felt his fist land square to the side of my face, sending me a couple feet backwards.

The Minotaur roared as he made his way to me. The sound of Death marched as my consciousness was fading yet again.

Thump. Thump. Thump.

"We're not so different Ollius, you fight to survive, I survive to fight."

He was getting closer, I didn't have much of a choice left, I had to rely on my rage yet again.

My light grew once again, lighting an ember in my eyes. I would not find myself a victim of this Arena.

I felt my body strengthen in pulses. The Colosseum was trying to strip away my everlasting fury. I had to make this one attack count, and I had to time it just right, if I didn't, it'd mean the end of my story.

I turned around, and in an instant, I stood from my knees, driving my silver blade through his gut—his blood landing on my wrist as the hilt pierced his insides.

It took everything out of me. Every ounce of strength I had was poured into one attack. The crimson light in my eyes faded as he fell to his knees, looking at me with woeful and regretted eyes.

He looked down; his muscular body tainted with his own blood for the first time.

He shed a tear before landing on his right side, his story meeting its end.

I looked all around me to see the victims of the Minotaur's slaughter slowly fade away. I granted them release, their deaths no longer meaningless.

One boy stood on the opposite side of the Arena, yet to fade. He wore black clothing, and his face was the only one of the spectators that were visible to the eyes.

I walked over, eager and worried about what the boy would bring with him. Was he an enemy, or maybe just another victim?

I reached for the wall, climbing to the top and entering the stands. It was time to meet my guest. His hair was a dark black, and his skin carried the same gray tone.

"Your friends are all dead, Ollius." The boy spoke, abruptly.

"What?"

"The Legion. They're all dead. King Illunus gave the order, and an army slaughtered every single one of them."

I was caught off guard, this seemingly innocent boy knew about the Legion and our plan to bring Sparta back. He was dangerous.

"How do you know that?"

The boy pointed to behind me where a man of thick heavy armor sat mere feet away from me.

Stergious.

"Whoa. How'd I miss you?" I asked as I patted him on his back.

"The boys right. I saw it with my own eyes Ollius. There was so much blood and slaughter. I can't believe I let it happen again." Sterg spoke, his voice breaking, tears falling down his face.

I reached over to embrace him as he welcomed my warm arms.

"Then we've got nothing to lose, Sterg. Come with me, we'll finish this together."

My heart broke. To get news that my home had been torn to pieces felt as if my heart had been ripped from my chest. Outside the Underworld, I had nothing to go back to.

Chapter 19: The Cerberus

We ventured outside the Arena, where the void was no longer in play. Across from me laid what looked to be dry tar. It was strong and had a yellow dotted line in the center of it. Mountains far past what the eye could see rose to strength, and a golden light spread through the wild, creating a reddish-orange landscape.

"I don't remember this." I said as I looked over to my side to see Stergious stand, a sad look on his face. His whole world was taken away, and he was left with nothing but another battle. To lose your home and family—how did he find the strength to keep walking alongside me? It was peculiar.

"How did you even get here?"

"I don't remember. There was a bright light, and I awoke in that Arena. I had to run for hours before I found my seat next to that boy. You remember that light too right?"

"Yeah. I remember."

That was the last time we spoke before we continued onto the road ahead of us. In the far reaches of the horizon, we saw what looked to be a palace. It had to mean what I thought it was.

That there was the home of Hades. Inside that palace was the man that terrorized my people for so long. I vowed to Nikolaus that I'd take his life a long time ago, and it was finally time that I brought that promise to fruition.

So, we walked for what seemed to be hours. Complete silence, accompanied by none other but our rage and misery.

We eventually did arrive to the door of the palace. It was menacing, in a word. Gigantic, and held up by pillars and other structures. It had more rooms than towns had homes. I opened the door to be greeted by nothing but silence. Inside was a mystery, one I was eager to solve.

I took my first step in to see a long humanoid creature in the center of the main room. It was gray and unnaturally long. Its limbs reached to the ground as its height peaked at over seven feet.

I heard rumbles of chains as Sterg removed his war hammer, charging towards the creature.

He sent the hammer down, crushing the creature—its bones breaking louder than its shrieks of pain.

He looked back to me, his eyes full of grief. He had lost the will to fight. His people were gone—his family unavenged, his story, untold. He was merely pushing for me to reach *my* goal—to avenge *my* people.

We climbed the stairs as creatures of the Underworld crept all around us. They attacked in the dozens at a time—all freakishly disfigured and horrifying. None stood to Sterg's hammer for more than a swing. He was a talented warrior and carried a horrifying strength alongside him. However, inside, his fire was extinguished. There was no ember left— only ashes and a dignifying smoke to remember a once-raging flame.

We continued climbing the palace, floor after floor, destroying creatures left and right. Supposedly, the Underworld was the center of all things evil. It was created with the sole purpose of tormenting damned souls, and yet we were breezing by as if it was child's play. How far had Hades fallen? He had let two Spartans invade the walls of his forgotten memories. Every single door we passed, every single step we climbed was built from the memories of the damned.

Door after door after another we broke down. We weren't sure of what we were looking for, only that it had to be high up.

So we climbed every step we saw as if chased by an arrow—and after climbing for so long we found ourselves at a brown wooden door. I jiggled the handle to no avail. I took a step back pondering on the best way to make it to the other side. I looked to the side window walking towards it and looking out. There was another window that we could climb to, but not with the risk of falling to our death.

"Sterg—"

I was interrupted by a loud bang behind me. He had broken through the door like a mad man.

"Come on," Sterg said before stepping inside.

Why didn't I think of that?

It was dark and smelled ancient as if nobody had stepped foot in here for eons. There was dust and cobwebs on every corner. It was a gigantic cube with three stones in the center like pillars.

On the top of every stone fragment, there was a golden bowl, with an inscription on the inside.

Blood of the traitor.

Blood of the pawn.

Blood of a God.

I looked to Sterg who looked back at me. He reached his palm out, offering it to my silver blade.

"What are you doing?"

"Blood of a traitor. Take it."

I said nothing for a few moments, pushing it away.

"I'm not doing that."

He grabbed me from my maroon collar, throwing me to the ground.

"This is no time to be pretentious—this is life or death! He must pay!" Sterg screamed as he held me down.

"What have you done?!" I screamed back.

"I can't tell you! Just take the blood!"

I turned Sterg to his side, kicking him off me.

Sterg landed on his back, rolling through the kick.

"This isn't time to be pretentious, and it isn't time for secrets. You need to tell me what you did—now." I said as I stood to my feet, standing over him with cold red eyes.

"I cost us everything! It was me, Ollius! I cost us everything!" Sterg shouted, tearing up.

"What do you mean?"

"I killed him, Ollius. The man that took my family—I tore his neck to shreds. I tore his arms off—and that's what led Greece to us. That careless act of unearned redemption cost us everything! I got so lost in the past, I forgot that I had a future—that we had a future. I'm sorry, I'm so sorry." I felt him let go of the tension inside his heart—it was never the loss of his family that haunted him, it was the monster inside him that brought out his forgotten silence.

I said nothing, walking over to him and ripping his palm into two, filling the bowl and setting it back down.

I walked over to the second bowl, letting my palm loose from all the blood I worked so hard to keep inside. All that was left was the Blood of a God.

We didn't have one—but I assumed I'd fit the criteria.

As I let out a drop of blood into the bowl, I saw it evaporate as it touched the bowl.

Suddenly, I felt weak, and my arm grew numb. I felt the world around me spin as I fell to my knee. I looked to my right arm to see an arrow stick out of it.

It carried a divine aura alongside it, as if fog to a storm.

"Sterg—" I said as I fell to my side.

He ran over to me, ripping the arrow out as soon as he could.

"Stay with me. Stay strong—Sparta needs you." Sterg said as he grabbed my head, raising it off the ground.

He looked to the arrow, noticing the divine aura smoke out of the tip.

"Blood of a God," Sterg said as I felt my strength return to me—although I was still weak,

"What are you saying?" I spoke, still lost in thought.

"This is the Blood of Demeter—it can poison anything. This is what we need."

"I don't understand."

"You don't need to. Just save your strength, I can take it from here."

Sterg let go of me, walking over to the bowl and breaking the arrow in two, dropping it in.

I sat up as the whole room shook. I felt the ground beneath me scream, yearning for escape. *What was coming?*

To my left, I saw the wall come crumbling down.

Darkness, overshadowed by silence stepped out.

A growl came from across the shadow. I felt something in my spine—*was it fear?*

"I think we should go," I said as I stood up, reaching for his shoulder.

"We can't—the doors locked, remember?" He returned.

"I don't know, I didn't check."

Sterg looked to me, at a loss for words.

"You didn't check?"

The creature roared, escaping into the bare light of the torches that stood on the walls.

"Get to the door Ollius, now!" Sterg said as he pushed me forward.

It was a three-headed black hound—Vassilios told me stories about this creature: *The Cerberus*.

It has a red collar, and a yellow light that beamed through their eyes—although their light alternated from bright to dim every second through the three creatures.

Sterg dragged me from the back of my shirt throwing me to the door as he blocked the jaw of one of the hounds.

"Go! Now!" He screamed at me.

"I can't leave you here!" I replied, breaking down to my knee once again.

"I'll be fine! Go!"

Chapter 20: The Chirps

I could hear the Cerberus bark in the near distance as the door shut behind me, muffling the sound.

I breathed a sigh of relief, having escaped what could've been certain death. I faced the wooden door, my arm in echoes of pain as I slid down to my knees, shedding a tear. I was in excruciating pain, and it had nothing to do with the arrow that pierced the back of my arm.

"You made it." I heard behind me.

It was a familiar voice, but not that of Hades. It was raspy and friendly.

It clicked in my head who it was. My eyes shot open as I turned my head slowly towards the figure that stood in the shadows.

He was skinny, and a little short, wielding a gigantic blade on his back.

"What?" I asked as I stood to my feet.

"You made it, Ollius." The voice spoke, walking out of the dark carrying a cup of whiskey in his right arm.

I felt dizzy. My entire world came to a stop as I realized who it was. The man that stood before me had been the person I trusted the most. He was there from the beginning; he was there to fight—but more importantly to protect me. He saved me from the shackles of loneliness.

"Hermaeus. What're you doing here?" I asked as I picked my jaw up off the floor.

"I'm afraid you know the answer." He replied, downing the cup of whiskey and throwing it to his side.

"It can't be—"

"Stop it." He interrupted me, his face no longer carrying the familiar smile I knew and loved.

"I don't understand!—"

"You don't need to. It doesn't change the fact that you won't leave this room alive Ollius of Sparta.

This is where you fall, and where I can finally bring truth to my revenge."

I broke down, back to my knees. My heart felt as if it had stopped. I hated the way my brain was screaming at me—I hated the way my heart made me feel. I felt my world crumble, I felt my fists shake. I was betrayed, a pawn to his game, a slave to his bidding. My best friend, the one person I thought I could always rely on, played me like a fool.

My rage grew to an overwhelming amount. It soared through the skies, calming the Cerberus in the previous room, it flew through the walls of the palace invading the rooms one by one igniting the flames long extinguished. The ground shook beneath me as I felt myself lose control—as if a captain of a ship with a broken wheel. I felt my consciousness lift, leaving me with an empty shell of chaos. There were no more roses left to grow—only ones to wither. They wanted me to become a monster, I was only following their directions. I left my cage, and broke through the shackles of greed and lust just to be left with a tear in my eye. All the blood I shed, none of it was my own, but I was the only one with tainted hands in every room I stood in. I was the only one with blood that would not wash off—I was the only one with skeletons in a closet I built.

I tried so hard, from the beginning to stand as an equal. I never wanted anything more—I just wanted to exist. I wanted my freedom just to find that deception was a far stronger ecstasy. I couldn't breathe in that moment, I only found myself vomiting. I felt nauseous, and my knees grew weak. My head was so loud with thoughts of violence and hate. My palms stank of unfiltered chaos.

Why Hermaeus? I've lost everyone I've ever known at this point. The Legion was in pieces— Vassilios had been murdered by me—Stergious had met his end to the Cerberus. Herm was all I had left in this world. He was my best friend and I trusted him with every fiber of my being. *Why did it have to be you, Herm?*

"You deserve this, don't forget that. That power of yours, that crimson light marked you for death the day you were born—"

"Why did you do this?!" I shouted, interrupting him.

"The sins of the father, Ollius."

"Why me?! Why do it to me?! What did I do to deserve this?! What heinous act did I commit?! I've been dragged through Hell since the day I was born! I was designed for murder; I was designed for slaughter! I was given this power to do nothing but! Why me?! Why me?!" I shouted as I slammed my fists to the ground.

"You are far too young to understand—"

"Shut up! Don't give me that! I've gone through too much, I've lost too much! How much do I need to give up? How much are you going to take before you're satisfied, Hades?! I've fought tooth and nail since I left that cage! I've been forced to murder people that loved me! I've taken so many lives I can't forget their faces at night! I can't breathe half the time! I can't see, I can't think! My head is so loud—all with thoughts of chaos—and I just want to drown them out. I want the pain, the ache, I want it all to stop! I can't keep living like this! I can't see a happy ending for myself. I can't see a way this is all going to work out—but you need to pay!" I shouted before I tackled Hermaeus to the ground.

Tears overflowed from my eyes as they landed atop his. I pounded his face repeatedly as I screamed.

It all went dark. I'm not sure what happened in those few moments where I lost control, only that I woke to a sharp pain in my right side.

My eyes lost their flame in that moment. I only felt the weight of Herms blade on my right shoulder, as he stood meeting me eye to eye. I lost the battle to Hades—he had won.

I fell to my back, hitting my head on the floor on my way down.

"Goodbye, Ollius. This is where your race ends."

I grabbed my right side as I felt my blood pour out.

The words of the Sage came rushing back to me, *every race has its end, even yours.*

"The Sage too?" I said as I coughed, sending blood into my palm.

"Afraid so." Hades replied, standing atop me.

"I trusted you, Herm. I trusted you."

Hades smiled, before his blade grew hot, forcing him to drop it.

Hades fell to a knee, grabbing his head as if trying to stop it from bloating.

I reached to grab his blade as I felt it connect to my wrist. An excruciating pain shot through my entire right arm as I felt something sprout from within. It was a collar, or a bracelet I wasn't sure. It was a beautiful rose gold color, and it swallowed the blade, mechanically folding inside the sphere.

I forced myself up as I walked over and fell atop Hades.

"I told you—you'd suffer a coward's death Hades." I said through sips of pain, anger radiating from the deepest part of my soul.

"Ollius. Hurry."

I felt the blinding rage subside as I came back to reality.

"Hurry up, I don't know how long I can hold him in here." Herm forced as he opened his eyes to meet mine.

"Herm?" I said as I felt my strength loosen.

"Do something!" Herm pleaded as he grabbed the collar of my maroon shirt. I heard the fabric stretch as his exhausted muscles forced me to reality.

"Herm—or Hades? Who are you?!" I shouted as I grabbed his wrists, forcing them away from my shirt.

"It's me! I lost control after I used the Gem against the army. This was his plan all along! I can hear him even now! If you don't kill me, he's going to kill Nikolina and make me watch! Ollius, I'm begging you!"

"I can't! I can't kill you, Herm! You're my best —"

"You have to set me free! Don't let him take control again. I can't watch her die, Ollius. I can't."

"How much more do I need to give up? How much more do I need to lose?!"

"The Legion is fine; the kid was lying! You have people waiting for you—but this is the end for me—my road ends here! You can't change that! Let me do one last thing for Sparta—for my people, before my name is erased from history. I'm begging you Ollius—do me this last favor." Herm plead as he grew a tear in his eye.

"Take my blade. It's yours. It's always been. I love you, friend."

I raised my wrist to the sky, the blade poking out before shooting up. I grabbed it as I placed it above Herm's heart. My hand shook as I realized this would be our last few moments together.

"I'll never forget you. Thank you, for everything."

"No, Ollius. Thank *you*. I would not have the strength to do this without you. Take care of Lina for me—and make sure to tell everyone I killed Hades, that Hermaeus of the Legion overpowered a God."

I drove my blade down, and the crunch of his ribcage filled the air as his scream rid the room of any mercy. The Beast of Baylor struck again—peaking onto his mountain of corpses was the remains of his best friend—yet no emotion or regret ran down his spine.

This was normal for him.

The beast only took—it never gave.

A croak spoke through Herm's neck, releasing his final breath to the world.

Releasing Hermaeus from the arms of life.

The rest was a blur. I fell to my back, but not before the entire realm shook. Hades was gone, and the transfer of power meant Persephone was on the rise.

I felt my eyes lose their light. My rage was finally to an end. A sense of relief and mourning took hold instead. As I looked up to the ceiling, I saw a mirror. My eyes were no longer glowing—my rage was finally satisfied.

Was this the end for me too? Was this how my race was destined to finish? Lying on the cold hard ground of a palace of the Gods?

For what a race it was and what a path I've ventured.

Alongside my best friend, I laid bleeding out. The stain on the carpet below forever eternalized today's sacrifice.

Forever remarking Hermaeus of the Legion.

A fitting end—my voice finally my own, my rage finally ceasing, my head finally quiet; I could see the trap door a lot more clearly now, for it was never locked, only forgotten.

Printed in Great Britain
by Amazon

81010977R00212